Pink Slip

The Spies Who Loved Her

Katrina Jackson

pink slip

Editor: Aretha Kaitesi Tibandebage

katrina jackson

content warnings

graphic descriptions of violence
deaths on- and off-page
maiming

prologue one: Lane
three years ago

When Lane was a teenager, he thought he'd be a baseball player. He was a solid pitcher, could catch a ball and had a pretty good eye for stealing bases, because he liked to show off. At fourteen those seemed like all the skills he'd need to make it to the majors.

But then his father got a new job and moved their family to D.C. and whatever trajectory his life had been on shifted dramatically. Which isn't to say that he would have played ball professionally if they'd stayed in Texas. He wouldn't. But after the move, all the things he'd once cared about felt like a million miles away and baseball became the least of his priorities. His family's cross-country move to the Capitol precipitated the worst few years of his life. But he survived them, graduated from high school, and then packed all of his few belongings, including the old stack of Dodgers baseball cards his father had given him – some time before he'd left his wife and two kids for his secretary like the absolute piece of shit he was – and he vowed to never return to D.C. if he could help it for the rest of his life. He hadn't really wanted to go to college, but he'd needed to put as much distance as he could between him and his trifling father, and his broken mother. College was just a place to be for a while as he tried to figure out what to do with himself next. But then he met Monica during his junior year and the trajectory of his life as an aimless frat boy shifted again.

They were in an intro Political Science course that they both hated and transferred out of immediately. But options were limited, and they clearly had similar schedule restrictions because when he walked into the Introduction to Criminology course, he recognized her immediately, and sat in the open seat behind her as if compelled.

Throughout the semester, Lane didn't think much about Monica while sitting behind her in class twice a week, besides that she was fucking beautiful and it seemed odd that a girl who scowled as much as she did always smelled like peaches. It was such a happy and bright scent for someone who seemed to be neither. And he might have gone on not thinking much about her if she hadn't saved his life.

There's nothing like drunkenly walking home from the pizza place just across the street from campus, almost getting mugged and then having the girl you vaguely have a crush on show up in her campus security outfit and scare the shit out of your would-be muggers to help you reset your life's priorities. Maybe it was a little bit of hero worship. Or maybe it was that, after two years of getting drunk at frat parties on weekends and fucking whoever seemed interested, while managing to eke by on a bottom of the barrel GPA, Lane only realized as he looked at Monica that he hadn't learned anything of use in college. Because how was he a junior and only just discovering that he had a thing for a woman in uniform? And as Monica walked him back to his room in the campus co-op housing dorm where he lived without ever speaking more than two sentences ("Are you okay? Do you want to create an incident report?"), Lane also realized that the strong and silent type did it for him. In a big way.

What followed were a few really pathetic months of him running after Monica and her not giving him the time of day. He preferred not to remember that time in their relationship. Monica brought it up constantly. He had been just about to give up on pursuing her and chalk his infatuation up to the lingering effects of the adrenaline spike during his near mugging, when he saw Monica rip a flyer from a message board in the International Affairs building for an internship program with the CIA.

He ran after her, knowing instinctively that this was his chance. "So the CIA, huh? You thinking of signing up?" His Texas drawl was normally just added a faint lilt to his words by this point in his life, but he made it a bit thicker since he liked to play it up with girls he was interested in. Not that it had worked on Monica thus far.

"You don't just sign up to the CIA. Stop stalking me," she replied matter-of-factly.

"I'm not stalking you. We have class together."

She turned to him then and looked him up and down as if to confirm his identity.

"Are you shitting me? I sit behind you twice a week."

"I don't turn around in class. My education is important to me, so I pay attention to lectures. Which is more than I can say for you."

Lane's eyebrows knit together. "If you don't turn around, then how do you know if I pay attention or not?"

She opened her mouth to speak and then snapped it shut. She stopped walking and turned to look at him. Lane wanted to laugh. He had her. He knew it. But as he watched the frustration play over her face, he figured that this was a delicate moment. It wasn't clear if the frustration he was seeing was with him or herself, but he could bet that for someone who had, for half the semester, only displayed one singular emotion – focus – she probably hated that she had given herself away so easily. So for once in his life he stayed quiet.

And twenty years later, he was damn happy that he had. Even if keeping his trap shut that day in the quad had directly led to the circumstances that had him hanging off of the side of a garbage truck on a hot early spring day in suburban Trenton, the stench of the refuse having long since burned away every hair in his nostrils.

Lane banged on the side of the truck, signaling to the driver to stop.

He checked the address and the house's exterior, confirming that they were finally at the target's house and if their intel was correct, it would be empty. But he could never be too careful.

He and the other agent hanging off the truck's sides jumped down and grabbed the trash cans from the curb to empty them into the waste collector. Lane took the now empty cans up the short driveway of the middle class pre-fabricated mansion, which was definitely the best house on the block. At the gate leading to the backyard he reached over the top and unlocked it, shaking his head at a man alleged to have accepted close to $3 million from the Russian mob who didn't have the brains to buy a fence tall enough to at least make breaking into his house somewhat of a challenge.

Once he'd slipped into the backyard, Lane set the trash cans down, stripped off the dingy coveralls of his disguise and placed them on the cans. Underneath, he wore a very unremarkable pair of jeans and a plain white t-shirt.

"In the yard," he said just loud enough to be heard.

"Good. Hurry up," Monica said, her voice coming through the transmitter into his ear.

"Do you want this done fast? Or do you want this done right?"

"I've been telling you for twenty years that the answer is both," she said. He could hear the playful note in her voice that most people missed.

He smiled but didn't respond. He needed to concentrate, and they needed to keep their chatter to a minimum.

"Security system?" he asked as he leaned around the corner of the house to peer through the large floor-to-ceiling windows that separated the backyard from a spacious chef's kitchen.

"State of the art. Can't hack it externally. When you set it off, you need to get to the control panel immediately and manually connect the decrypting device. I'll reroute the company's call and buy you some time."

"How much?"

"Six minutes max. So work fast."

"Yes, ma'am."

pink slip

The sliding door was locked. Lane pulled a lock-picking set from his back pocket and bent down. He almost wished that the lock had been harder to pick. But he also wasn't a man who enjoyed taking unnecessary risks. He had a good life and being a spy wasn't the most important part of it. There was no adrenaline rush in the world that would be worth losing one minute with Monica.

When he pulled the sliding door open he expected to hear a blast of sound. But the house was eerily quiet and he stopped a few steps into the kitchen.

"Silent alarm. Move," Monica demanded in the hard tone that Lane loved.

Lane had memorized the house's schematics and turned to his right. He pushed open the pantry door and located the security panel behind it. He pulled the decrypting device from his back pocket and slid the connective cord into a small port underneath the panel that most people would miss.

"In," he announced simply.

He held his breath, listening to the still quiet house and waiting for Monica's reply.

"I'm in. Six minutes," she stated.

He disconnected the device and took off quickly but cautiously through the kitchen and then down the front hallway to the office. He tamped down on the feeling that this was too easy. He wasn't new to this. Most rookies thought every mission was a battle and if it wasn't, they assumed it must be a trap. Lane had been young and dumb once, following Monica into The Agency like the lovesick puppy he was. But after a particularly bloody takedown of a German double agent that left him with a few broken ribs, a concussion and some sprained fingers because he'd let the other man goad him into an old-school fist-fight rather than neutralize him as he should have, Monica had put her foot down. "I'm not marrying a man with a death wish. So if you want to be with me, you need to act like you want to live." Lane had been so distracted by the forcefulness with which she'd said so many words at him all at once that it had taken a while for those words to sink in.

Now they were in his bones. Her voice overrode every Agency protocol, every mission directive and every biological instinct. Monica said he had to come home to her; so he did.

He took a cloning device from his other pocket and connected it to the computer tower. He knew the target's log-in but not the password. The agency's hackers had given him some options that he mentally filtered through in his head. He disregarded the totally random options because any man who had such a low fence and a standard lock on his exterior doors was likely cocky as hell and had not bothered to create an elaborate or difficult-to-crack password. And soon enough he was going to regret it.

It took Lane three tries (wife, daughter, son) before he got it: Adam82005; the target's son's name and birthdate. He shook his head in disgust. Barely even a challenge. Once the computer was unlocked, he began downloading the hard drive. He checked his watch and noted that he still had just over four minutes. So it was about time that something went wrong.

Lane's heart sped up when he heard the front door open. By the sound of the shoes and the fast, squirrelly pace of the footsteps, he knew it was the target. He pushed the office door closed silently and pressed himself against the wall behind it. The sound of his blood was racing in his ears. His eyes darted to the computer screen; the download was halfway completed.

When the door opened, the target didn't have enough time to register the scene on his desk before Lane put him in a headlock. He struggled for a few minutes, then released a spurt of energy that was pure panic as he realized that there would be no relief. Lane kept his grip strong and calmly waited for the target to drift into unconsciousness.

"ETA?" Monica's voice invaded his ear as he was pulling the target onto the couch across the room.

pink slip

When he seemed settled, Lane went to the target's bar, filled a tumbler with whiskey and then put the glass into the target's hand, pressing his fingers around the glass. He released his hold and watched the liquid splash onto the carpet, followed by the glass. Intel indicated that the target was a mostly high-functioning alcoholic. The scene set; he went back to the desk. "Twenty seconds," he said, finally answering Monica.

She didn't answer, but he knew her well enough to know that her lips were probably set in a hard line and she'd nodded, even though he couldn't see it. The computer dinged. The download was complete.

"Done," Lane said and disconnected the cloning device. He closed the office door behind him and sprinted across the kitchen. He pushed the sliding door closed and headed out of the backyard the way he'd come. He grasped the coveralls but didn't put them on. He walked briskly down the street, stripping the latex gloves from his hands, the garbage truck in his line of sight. When he was close, he crossed the street behind the truck and tossed his coveralls and gloves into the waste receptacle and nodded surreptitiously to the other agent - a sign that the mission was done and now it was time to scatter.

"On my way," he said as he turned off the target's street. There was an old black sedan Monica had parked here the evening before, specifically for his getaway.

"Good. Now hurry up and get to The Warehouse. We're interviewing another assistant."

Lane let out an exasperated breath as he folded his long, lanky body into the front seat. "Can't we just let The Agency hire one?"

"We did that last time," Monica reminded him. "He almost got us both killed with dry cleaning."

"Fine. But I'm running home to shower. I can still smell that damn garbage truck on me."

"I was just about to suggest that." Lane heard the smile in her voice. "I'll meet you there," she said. "Love you."

"Love you too, boss."

"Don't drive too fast," she said and disconnected the line.

Just as Lane pulled onto the interstate, he manually rolled down the driver's side window, snatched the receiver from his ear, tossed it out onto the highway and sped off.

prologue two: Monica
three years ago

Monica liked things done her way. She liked her files in order, every book in its place and she wanted her to-do list executed to her very particular specifications.

From the first time she'd ever laid eyes on Lane his presence had disrupted the order she craved. But that moment was not, as he remembers, the night he was almost mugged, or sitting in front of him in Intro to Criminology, or even before that in the Political Science class they'd both dropped after one day.

It was two months prior. She was an incoming first year student, on campus to meet with her new academic advisor, register for classes and get to know the campus. But Monica already knew the campus like the back of her own hands. Her father had worked as a campus security officer her entire life.

He'd come to the Bronx from Puerto Rico when he was eighteen, met Monica's mother through family friends a year later when he was still doing odd jobs around the neighborhood for spare money while he worked on his accent – since his uncle had stressed, even before he'd bought her father's plane ticket to the US, that the thicker his accent, the lower his paycheck. From the moment he'd met Monica's mother, he'd taken whatever menial job he was offered and saved every penny in a bid to prove that he would do anything to take care of her and their future children. He was hired as a janitor for the university, married Monica's mother three months later and a year after that he started as a probationary campus security officer. Monica's father was her own personal embodiment of the American promise that hard work pays off.

That importance of hard work was Monica's most enduring memory of her childhood. Educational success mattered to Monica's parents, but for Monica or her two younger brothers to meet their standards, they had to put in the work. If Monica brought home an A on an exam that her parents hadn't observed her studying for, her mother would make this sound in the back of her throat, as if tsk-ing at the fickleness of luck. But if she brought home a B for an exam, she'd spent every waking hour preparing for, her father would attach it to the fridge with a magnet as if it were the Nobel Prize. Because luck runs out, but hard work is its own reward.

So Lane was not the kind of boy she was looking for in college. Actually, she wasn't looking for any boy or girl in college; she didn't need the distraction. She was there to be the first person in her family to get a college degree, set a good example for her brothers, be recruited into the CIA and buy her parents the house they deserved so they could finally retire. Her mission was clear. But as she was wandering across the large green lawn at the center of campus, she'd seen him. He was lanky, lean muscle covered in skin bronzed by the summer sun. His straight, light brown hair was longer than she liked, almost touching his shoulders.

Her eyes scanned his body but then she looked away. She likely would have forgotten him, but then he spoke, his voice carrying over the humid summer air. His Southern accent was deep and playful and overly thick. It was an affectation. She could hear the stress he placed on dropping the endings of some words but not others. And she loved it.

She began to walk faster, hoping to get away from the feelings his voice stirred in her gut. She didn't have time for a white boy with a broad skinny chest, messing with her family's plans for her. And so of course he walked into her Poli Sci class on the first Tuesday of the semester. And of course, he'd shown up on Thursday in her Criminology class.

She spent half a semester looking as if she was paying close attention to their professor while she tried not to show how much attention she was paying to Lane. He became a singular point of disorder in her neatly ordered world, first just those two days a week and then every day. Until finally the whirlwind that he created became a familiar release from the predictability that ruled every other aspect of her life. And because she loved him, she accepted that. He reminded her that sometimes it was okay to go with the flow and see where you ended up. Where they ended up; together.

But working together had at times been difficult. At home, they could manage their differences, but over time their disparate personalities had begun to affect their work. They decided that they had two options: fix it or stop working together. Neither of them was willing to accept the latter so they'd agreed that hiring an assistant was the best course to mediate their differences. But they needed someone who could perform to her exacting standards, manage all of Lane's chaos and keep the peace between them professionally.

Monica was in the backseat of a chauffeured car. She was poring over the employment application and background check for the latest candidate to be their personal assistant. She was wearing a very professional pencil skirt that hit at a very respectable length just above the knee and a light knit jumper. The job ad had been purposefully vague about her and Lane's employment, so she was dressed generically as the wife of a diplomat or the wife of a politician on the campaign trail.

By any metric, Kierra Ward was not the candidate they needed. She did not have clearance, her student loan debt was a potential liability and she had no experience as a personal assistant. There were a whole host of better equipped assistants that were already Agency-approved. But every PA they'd been assigned so far had pissed off either Monica or Lane or, in the last instance, both of them. They were determined that whoever they hired had to be able to please them both and, for their own sanity, had to be someone they could envision working for them long-term.

The car came to a slow stop. Monica shoved the files from her lap into her shoulder bag and waited for the chauffeur to open her door. But when the door opened, Lane's large hand reached into the backseat to help her from the car. His lopsided, cocky grin greeted her as she stepped into the mild late afternoon air of late fall.

"How'd you get here before me?"

"I have my ways," was all he said before leaning in to press his lips to her cheek.

She smiled, remembered that there were other agents standing guard around them and frowned. "Have you read her file?"

Lane sighed dramatically, indicating that he had not.

He slipped the files from her hand and she turned to walk toward the abandoned warehouse that the Agency reserved for rendezvous with clients and contacts who had minimal or no clearance. Lane fell into step beside her, flipping through Kierra's file as they moved.

"A poet?"

"I know."

"That's a lot of debt," he said, picking up on all of Monica's concerns.

"I had more when I was recruited," she offered as a rebuttal.

They'd reached the back entrance to the building and Lane's hand shot out to grasp the door handle, but he didn't pull it open. She checked her watch. Five minutes before Kierra showed up.

"Let's say we hire her," he said, locking her in his stare. "Do you really think she'll stay for a few years? She has a master's in literature and fine arts, why would she want to be our PA for more than a few months?"

Monica nodded, "Let's ask her."

***

To the outside world Monica and Lane were nice, upper middle-class philanthropists. Their neighbors had been led to believe that they made their living traveling the world preaching the gospel of micro-lending as a business innovation with a clear moral imperative. In The Agency they were one of a handful of couples who blended espionage with their real personal lives – eschewing the extended deceit of a non-spy spouse, which always ended poorly. They weren't the only married spies, but they were currently the only couple who'd walked into the international spy racket already together. Company gossip was that they were definitive "hashtag relationship goals" as their first assistant, who left to train as an agent, used to tell them. And the reality was that they were all of those things and kinky.

Monica and Lane had been, since their third date, the kind of couple who were attached at the hip. Not because they needed to be, but because they wanted to be. There had been something intoxicating about finding each other when they were young and just beginning to experience their first taste of adulthood and all the mistakes it entailed, that made the earliest phases of their relationship feel like freedom personified. They allowed each other to think and say and feel everything without judgement and with the sure knowledge that they had someone there to share it all with.

And they had shared everything. And everyone.

Monica watched Kierra walk on scared legs, the blindfold firmly covering her eyes, her hand placed delicately on the driver's arm.

When she was near, Lane stood from his seat and helped the driver settle Kierra into the chair across the boardroom table separating Monica from her potential employee. It was a ridiculous thing to have an elegant formal oak table and office chairs in the middle of this cavernous seemingly abandoned warehouse, but Monica didn't bother to question it.

When Kierra was seated, the driver walked past them with a nod of his head for Monica. While they waited for him to exit, Monica's eyes locked on Lane.

He had that cocky grin playing on his lips again.

Kierra jumped at the sound of the door opening and then jumped again as it slammed closed.

"Hello," she said in a small, terrified voice.

Lane looked at Monica. She should speak. His voice would terrify her. What woman would want to find herself in a room, blindfolded, with a strange man? But Monica's tongue felt thick and immobile in her suddenly dry mouth. Kierra smelled like lavender and it did something unexpected to her core.

She cleared her throat. Kierra jumped.

"Hello," she said again.

"Calm down, Ms. Ward," Monica finally said. She'd meant the words to sounds soothing, but they came out like a barking command. Monica would have apologized except that Kierra had shivered at her words.

Monica nodded to Lane to remove the blindfold. Kierra's hands went straight to her hair, smoothing her strands back into place. Monica found that unconscious vanity oddly endearing. She turned to see Lane behind her, her eyes widening in obvious fear. And then she turned back, locking eyes with Monica.

"Hello, Ms. Ward. My name is Monica Peters, and this is my husband, Lane." Peters was their comfortable alias, the one they used for their almost-personal lives.

"Hi," Kierra replied in a small, shy voice, her eyes immediately settling on Monica's lips. And then she cleared her throat and said in a much stronger voice this time, "Hello. It's nice to meet you both." This time she settled her gaze a bit higher on the bridge of Monica's nose.

Monica clenched her hands into fists but hid them under the table in her lap.

"Thank you for making time in your day to meet with us," Monica said.

The words seemed to pull Kierra back into the moment and remind her why she was here.

17

pink slip

She sat up straight and nodded towards them. "No, thank you. I really appreciate the opportunity."

"So, tell us a little about yourself, darlin'," Lane said casually, his voice oozing an innocence that Monica knew was a put on. She had to dig her nails into her palms at the way he said 'darlin'".

That voice, low and careless, was classic misdirection. It put the women and men they invited into their bed at ease. He'd lay that accent on thick and call them 'darlin'", 'sweetheart' and sometimes 'pumpkin', weaving a whole Southern fantasy with that easy grin and relaxed posture.

Monica was sympathetic. She could close her eyes and remember the first time she'd fallen under his spell. She was by no means immune to it now, but over the years she had become used to feeding off of the promises buried beneath that soft burr he used to seduce their playmates. But she still had to gird herself against that same voice trying to convince her to leave the office early or be a bit reckless in the name of a little fun. And at night, she had to hold that voice at bay while he asked her so damn gentlemanly to fuck him faster or say his name louder or to eat their new friend harder. It was a battle because she was in charge and Lane just loved testing the bounds of her control.

That voice was not for work. It wasn't even for company unless she said so. Calling Kierra 'darlin'" was another one of those challenges that Monica tolerated because they made her wet.

Monica tried to focus on what Kierra was saying but only snatches filtered through her growing lust. Instead her attention was centered on the way Lane's legs were spread wide so that his right knee was bumping into her crossed legs. Just to aggravate her.

He took over the interview; asking the questions from their agreed upon script. Nothing alarming stood out in Kierra's answers, Monica thought, although again her brain wasn't that invested in her biggest weakness or conversely her biggest strength. Instead she was thinking about how much she liked the sound of Kierra's voice and the way Kierra's head swiveled between her and Lane as she answered his questions; her eagerness to please them both equally clearly evident. Monica's sex kept clenching as Kierra's earrings bounced when her head moved.

And then Lane's voice cut through the haze. "That all seems well and good, sweetheart. But you'll be working for both of us and we're very different. I'm easy, very laidback," he said.

Monica rolled her eyes, which Kierra caught. She giggled and then covered her mouth quickly with one hand. She apologized silently with wide, rich, beautiful brown eyes.

"No need to apologize," Lane said, his hand reaching out under the table to settle on Monica's knee because he knew that after that giggle, she'd need him to keep her grounded.

"So, like I was saying, I'm the easy one. And my wife is demanding, with very exacting standards, and maybe sometimes just a bit hard to please."

Monica licked her lips, her eyes trained on Kierra's nipples which seemed to have hardened as Lane spoke.

"So my question," he asked, "is how you'd work to please both of us?" He emphasized the word 'both'.

And then Kierra sighed. It was a light exhalation, full of pleasure and promise and yearning that Monica might have missed if her entire being hadn't been taut with tension, hanging on Kierra's every breath. Monica never heard her answer. She didn't care.

And then the interview was ending. The driver had returned, ready to take Kierra back to the car and drive her home. Lane reached his hand out to shake Kierra's hand. And then it was Monica's turn. When their skin touched, Kierra unconsciously licked her lips and Monica's eyes dropped to savor the movement. She bit her own lips and stared at that flash of tongue. Lane's hand settled on the small of her back. Monica pulled her hand away reluctantly.

pink slip

"We still have a few more interviews, Kierra. But I think this has been a good experience. Very good," he said and then kissed Monica's cheek. Again, the way Monica might have responded to that very unprofessional show of affection changed completely at Kierra's reaction; her eyes tracking Lane's lips brushing across Monica's skin.

"I agree," Monica said. Kierra nodded slowly, her eyes on them for a second too long before skittering away. She finally turned abruptly to leave. Still on shaky legs.

They stood there, watching Kierra walk away, Lane's hand tight around Monica's waist. And then Lane unexpectedly yelled after her. "You'll hear from us real soon, sweet girl."

Monica closed her eyes and let her head fall back, her body physically unable to handle the way he said, 'sweet girl', as if those two words were a filthy promise of everything they wanted to do to her.

Because of course they were.

PART ONE

one
today

Kierra stood in front of her full-length mirror in a black lace bra and a matching pair of panties, considering her outfit options.

What does one wear to start their last week of work?

She considered something very professional that she knew her boss, Monica Peters, would love. She slipped on a white button-down shirt and shimmied into a black, skin-tight jersey pencil skirt. She could lean into the look with a sleek ponytail, minimal makeup, and a pair of four-inch black platform Mary Janes. The very thin heel would be impractical and just barely professional, but Monica would appreciate Kierra's commitment to the aesthetic. She lifted onto the balls of her feet and turned around to admire the way her ass looked in the skirt.

She pulled off this first choice and slipped into a pair of tight, skinny black leather trousers and a cropped band t-shirt. She could pair this look with her favorite Doc Martens, an excess of chunky silver jewelry, a bold, colorful eye look, and a lipstick just begging to be smudged. This option would be right up her boss, Lane Peters', alley: unprofessional, if not downright anti-authority.

Her cell phone beeped and she walked to the bed to look at it. The alarm notification reminded her that it was time to stop fucking around and get going. She needed to pick up the Peters' coffee and set up for their morning debrief.

She turned back to the mirror and decided, as she usually did, to compromise. She swapped out the pants for the pencil

22

skirt. She considered the Doc Martens, but slipped on a pair of heels instead. Not the four-inch platforms that would make Monica's stoic face break for a fraction of a second, but a dark brown patent leather pair that matched her skin perfectly and would appeal to Lane's love of long legs and an almost dangerously thin heel.

She fluffed her shoulder-length wavy black hair, pulled it into a half ponytail, swiped a berry-toned lipstick over her lips that accentuated the red undertones of her skin and then a super shiny clear gloss over top of it. She grabbed her bag and breezed out of her front door seconds before her alarm began to blare that it was absolutely time for her to leave for work.

It was strange to think that she only had a few more days to pick up Monica and Lane's coffee on the way to work, extra hot so that it was the perfect temperature when she arrived. Just a few more days to flounce around the office on her too high, too skinny heels in an outfit that was too tight or too short, or both, desperately putting herself on display for them. She only had five more days to spend her lunch break locked in the bathroom no one besides her ever used and slowly finger herself while she recalled every one of their scrutinizing stares, gentle but firm instructions (Lane) and restrained commands (Monica). But she wouldn't let herself come; she never did. It gave her a particular thrill to sit in their office, knees together, pussy wet and trembling, while they all went over the next day's schedule in excruciating, somehow erotic detail.

She only had one more week with them. And she wanted to savor every minute.

On her very last Friday as Monica and Lane Peters' personal assistant, she wanted to come home as she usually did, barely wave at her best friend and roommate, Maya, and then lock herself in her bedroom with her favorite vibrator. She wanted to dive into the release of as many orgasms as she could handle after hours teetering on the brink, images of her

pink slip

(former) bosses clouding her brain and their names falling like a chant from her lips.

Because all good things must come to an end.

Apparently.

Monica

Monica's body was tense. She was standing erect, her back straight, her legs shoulder-width apart with a light escrima stick in each hand. Her face was hot, and she could feel beads of sweat dribbling down her back. Her senses were acute and focused on Lane. She was waiting.

He was facing her, rolling on his feet from his heels up to his toes, reminding her that even though he was a few years older than her, his body was still light and agile. Lane was wearing the easy smile that Monica had long since learned to ignore because she knew that it didn't mean anything. Instead, she let her eyes travel over his face, cataloging the flare of his nostrils as he breathed, the crow's feet at the corners of his eyes and between his eyebrows and his biggest tell of all: his bright red ears.

If his cheeks had been a bright crimson, that would have indicated his embarrassment or discomfort. If that blush had spread down his neck in splotches, she would have deduced that he was angry. But only his ears turned red when he was horny.

"You gonna make a move, old man?" she asked in a whispered challenge.

"When I'm ready," he said. "And you're not gonna goad me into anything like I'm a young bull."

"That's what you always say," she said, shifting her weight from one foot to another.

He didn't move his head, but she knew that his eyes had tracked the movement. She'd lightly twisted her ankle on a mission to Portugal a month ago. It had long since healed, but she wanted him to wonder if she was still favoring it.

He laughed, "You told me your ankle felt fine."

She didn't answer him.

"How much time we got?"

She had to force her eyes not to shift to the clock on the wall to her left. If he wanted to know the time, then he could let his guard down and look.

He didn't.

"You gonna answer me?"

"Is your plan to talk me to death with that thick ass accent you think makes my pussy wet? Because that might actually work."

"Oh yeah?" That easy smile raised into a self-satisfied grin.

"Yep. You keep on talking and I'll fall right to sleep."

He grunted a laugh.

"Come on, darlin'," she said, imitating his accent. "Let's play."

His body tensed as the word 'play' left her mouth. "Are we playing? Is that what we're doing?"

She smirked but didn't speak. She saw his body shift to his left foot, and he lunged toward her. She held her sticks up to defend herself against his. They both retreated and began walking in a circle, studying one another.

"That was nice," she said, wanting to annoy him. "You got any more? Or do you need a break?"

He smiled and struck out at her as he spoke, "I can go all day, all night. You know that."

Monica blocked Lane's sticks, skirted to the left and then reached around to drop one arm and tap him lightly on his ass with the stick in her hand. "That's one," she said and then skipped backward out of his reach.

He only grunted in response. But then he leaned forward to crouch down, eyeing her across the mat like prey.

Monica's nipples hardened at the sight, but her voice was light. "Are we getting serious now?"

"Nope," he said, "still playing."

She thought he would lunge, but he stood up straight again and locked eyes with her.

"I hope she wears something short today," he said, waiting for her eyes to glaze over before striking. Her response was sluggish, and she could only back away, but not far enough. He tapped her on the right arm and left hip simultaneously. "Two."

Monica was pissed. And horny. "That was low," she hissed.

And then he laughed. "No, that V-neck t-shirt she wore last week was low. And she just kept leaning over my shoulder all day. Trying to get your attention."

It was Monica's turn to strike. Their sticks crashed together. "Flirt," she said.

Lane crouched, pushing his shoulder into her stomach and grabbing her around the knees. Monica's sticks fell from her hands when her back hit the mat. She reached down to wrap an arm behind the back of his neck and bent her knees. He grunted when she collided with his chest, but he held her tight enough to block her full blow.

They wrestled on the ground, pushing and grabbing at each other, fighting for dominance. When his hold on her legs was finally broken, she pushed against his chest and flipped him onto his back. She straddled his waist. His hard dick pressed into her covered mound.

"How much time do we have?" She asked the question this time, although the stakes of their activity had changed slightly.

"Depends," he replied. "You want to be in the office when she gets here? Or do you want me to fuck you, knowing that she's downstairs with your coffee, organizing all your files perfectly, just the way you like?" His hands fell to her waist and he ground his hips upward, pressing himself into her harder.

Monica moaned despite herself.

He sat up and grasped her behind the neck to pull her mouth to his.

pink slip

"What's it gonna be, boss?" The question was a thick tumble of drawled words, the rumble of his deep voice stroking her already excited pussy.

Monica licked her lips and tasted his sweat when it grazed the corner of his mouth. And then she remembered. "It's her last week." The words were like a bucket of cold water being tipped over them.

Lane's thumb smoothed soft circles on the skin at her hairline. "It doesn't have to be," he whispered, not for the first time in the four months since Kierra had handed in her notice. "We could ask her to stay."

She put her hands on his chest and tried to push him away. He tightened his grip on her. "No," she finally said. "We both know what she'd want if she stayed."

"And we both want to give it to her."

It wasn't that simple. Lane knew that. They'd been talking about it for three years. She opened her mouth to rehash this same argument for the hundredth time in as many days when their cell phones began to beep.

They pushed away from each other immediately. Lane sprang to his feet and offered her his hand. She ignored him and jumped to her feet. He shook his head and smiled at her affectionately. They walked to the edge of the mat, grabbed their phones and scanned the secured message there. The full mission brief would be available on The Agency's dark web site, but what they saw was enough to indicate that playtime was over.

two

Kierra pulled her car up to the large wrought iron security gate enclosing Monica and Lane's home, pressed her thumb and her middle finger (Lane's idea) onto the fingerprint scanner and then smiled nice and wide for the facial recognition scan. She knew there was a log of these photos somewhere and she always wanted to look her best for the Peters.

"Identity accepted," the digital voice announced.

"Thanks, doll," Kierra said with a wink at the machine, as always.

She parked her car in the large circular driveway, grabbed her purse and the coffee and took long strides to the front door that she knew would look sexy on the surveillance footage.

When Maya asked her about work, Kierra usually fabricated stories about running to the dry cleaner's or dog walking; anything that sounded even remotely like the other personal assistant jobs their friends had. Because no one would have believed her if she'd started talking about reviewing satellite surveillance, hours spent on the dark web tracing Bitcoin transfers and scheduling maintenance on the weapons vault. Besides, telling them any of that would have been a violation of the NDA she'd signed when the Peters hired her.

Kierra had literally stumbled into this job. She'd been a broke MFA graduate with no job prospects and no family to turn to for financial help, because unlike her classmates, she didn't come from money. Thankfully her mentors had prepared her for the life of a poet with hard truths. "Making ends meet might be difficult and you will often be simultaneously sad and full of joy," her mentor, Gwendolyn Miles, had drummed into her brain. "So plan accordingly."

pink slip

Signing up at an agency that specialized in providing personal assistants to the rich, famous, and powerful seemed like a bog-standard idea. She was an ideal candidate: well-organized, strong written and oral communication, a fast learner, and a team player. The few positions she'd interviewed for, but hadn't gotten, were quite normal. And then she'd interviewed with the Peters.

Kierra hadn't thought anything of signing an NDA to go on the interview but had raised an eyebrow when they sent along a release for a more thorough background check after. In hindsight, she should have realized that they were not politicians or diplomats, as she'd originally assumed. What politician sent a hired car to pick up a job candidate for an interview and then had the driver stop a few minutes from the interview location to put a blindfold on? What diplomat held a job interview in an abandoned airport hangar? Who called from an encrypted phone number to offer someone a job?

Sure, hindsight was 20/20 and she should have realized the kind of job she was accepting. But she wasn't quite in her right mind. Because the entire time she'd been sitting across from Lane and Monica Peters in an abandoned warehouse answering the most mundane of interview questions ever ("What would you say is your greatest strength? Conversely, what would you say is your greatest weakness?"), Kierra's pussy had been dripping wet. The mystery and excitement of it all had sent her adrenaline and lust spiking off the charts as soon as she'd laid eyes on Lane and then Monica.

So when they'd called to offer her the job, of course she'd said yes. She'd have been an idiot to turn that down.

The first few weeks had seemed like a probationary period through the looking glass, because nothing was as it appeared. Monica and Lane were still pretending to not be spies, speaking in code whenever Kierra was around, disappearing for days and having closed door meetings in the conference room they called "The Vault". Kierra had been obliviously filing paperwork and authorizing payments to contractors, too distracted by her own lust to wonder what kind of services A & P Plumbers could provide that would warrant a $200,000 bill. But one day Kierra had shown up to the Peters home, coffee in hand and an innocent smile on her face only to find Monica lying on the kitchen table, a gunshot wound in her side, and Lane bent over her prone form patching up the hole. Kierra, the daughter of a nurse, had finally realized that her sexy bosses were *definitely* not diplomats just before she noticed that Lane's stitches were uneven. She'd pushed him aside, fixed Monica's sutures and then the real fun began.

The Peters home was a small mansion in the Upper Montclair suburb of New Jersey. If one of their neighbors happened to stop by, which none did because of the very state-of-the-art security gate, they would have walked into a pristine and luxurious open plan front room, dining area and kitchen. All very modern. All virtually unused. Their home decor was so beautiful that most people would have found it hard to recognize that the dimensions were a little off. But without blueprints - which were classified anyway – no one would ever know for sure anyway.

Kierra walked through the kitchen, into the large pantry and lifted the small box of baking soda at the back of the second highest shelf. She felt around with her fingers until they grazed the latch that opened the wall in front of her. She kept a firm grip on the railing as she descended a short flight of stairs and walked, in her very skinny heels, into the real heart of the house. She liked to call it Command. Monica and Lane did not. But like a few things here and there over the past three years, they'd eventually caved to Kierra's enthusiasm and begrudgingly used the nickname.

Normal days were few and far between in this line of work, but she'd assumed that things would be light and breezy for her final week. Maybe it was her own lingering naiveté, but she walked in on that Monday morning with a very mundane to-do list for a PA/office assistant that consisted of some light filing, updating operational manuals

pink slip

for Monica, creating a detailed list of Lane's favorite local restaurants and scheduling the next few months of household bill payments from their joint cover account, to smooth the transition for them and whoever they hired to replace her. So she was not prepared when Monica rushed at her, grabbing the coffee from her hands.

"Do you have your passport?" Monica barked.

Kierra swallowed and clenched her thighs together, trying to focus. "Of course," she said. If Lane had asked the question, she would have fired back with something sarcastic about this not being her first day on the job and rolled her eyes. But Monica didn't like back talk, so Kierra responded accordingly.

Lane came around the corner in an easy stroll that contrasted sharply with his wife's determined gait and intense glare. He wore the languid smile on his face that Kierra had come to love, even though she was almost certain that it was a mask. But then his eyes truly lit up. "Coffee!"

Monica handed both cups to Lane who read the writing on the side of each like an overeager child before he located his double shot macchiato and took a happy sip.

"Turn around," Monica ordered.

Monica hated questions even more than she hated back talk, so Kierra turned slowly in her heels, tight skirt and cropped band t-shirt, that exposed just the tiniest sliver of skin at her ribcage. She bit her lip as she faced away from them, trying to calm herself at the thought that they were seeing how absolutely perfect her ass looked in this skirt.

"Perfect," was all Monica said as Kierra faced them again.

Kierra tried not to purr at the compliment; since she wasn't sure exactly what her look was perfect for.

"I hope you don't have any plans this week. We've got an assignment and you're coming with us."

At that, Monica turned to Lane. He offered her the other coffee cup and then she sped away. Kierra turned to Lane with dozens of questions surely reflected on her face.

"European dictator. We'll brief on the jet."

"You couldn't have told me this twenty minutes ago? I could have packed a bag."

"We'll buy you what you need when we arrive," he said, as if this was just a normal thing employers said to employees. Although, Kierra had to admit that this was pretty normal for them.

She let out an exasperated sigh and put one hand on her hip. "Fine. What do you need me to do?"

Lane took another slow sip of his coffee. Kierra tried not to ogle his lips on the lid. And then he said, in a serious tone, "Protocol Echo, Level 4. We're not sure what we're going to find when we land." He quirked his left eyebrow and raked his eyes down her body and then back up again. "I like the shoes," he said in his playful voice before walking away.

Alone in the foyer of Command, Kierra's mind raced through the Protocol Echo, Level 4 directives, starting a list of support equipment to pack and overseas resources to put on Monica's contact list, but it was hard to concentrate with her nipples hard enough to cut glass.

three

There are, unsurprisingly, a lot of perks to being the personal assistant to spies. First, the pay was absolutely insane. After three years working for the Peters, Kierra had paid off all of her student loans and saved enough money to register for a writing retreat in Enniskerry in County Wicklow in Ireland, travel for a year in West Africa like she'd always dreamed and still live comfortably while she tried to finish writing her first book of poetry. Sure, she had to route her paycheck through various shell companies controlled by the Peters – and maybe the U.S. government? – to disguise her actual salary and employer, but it was worth it. Especially since most of her friends were languishing in underpaid entry level positions.

Second, Kierra thought as she settled into a seat on the luxury executive private jet they always used for international travel, the Peters knew how to travel in style. Granted, they had to have their jet swept for bugs and explosives before boarding, and the entire crew had been subjected to background checks so thorough Kierra could tell them their fifth grade English teacher's names. And yea, they traveled under pseudonyms, with heavy encryption tools for all communications sent while in transit. But Kierra had never felt anything so lovely as the soft buttery leather of the jet's seats.

"Let's get down to business," Monica said, which was Kierra's signal to lock the door to the main cabin; an unnecessary precaution, but Monica always insisted on sticking as closely to protocol as possible.

When she sat back down, Lane handed her his tablet. The screen showed a picture of Miroslav Banović, Serbian dictator, who had been very openly threatening to commit genocide against the Muslim refugees settling in the east of his country.

"This is our target. We're heading to Novi Sad, Serbia's second largest city. He has a holiday home there that he only visits *without* his wife," Lane said.

Kierra nodded, understanding the implication. "So who is he fucking there?" she asked.

She looked up just in time to see Lane turn to Monica with a small nod and smile that she reciprocated. Kierra wanted to feel ashamed that this small gesture of their approval made her feel good. But after three years of running after every bit of praise they handed out, she had long since stopped admonishing herself for the way her skin warmed and her sex felt tight when she received it.

"There are a number of fetish clubs in the city that Banović likes to frequent," Monica responded. "They're not to his wife's tastes."

"Shame," Kierra said before she could stop herself and then she pursed her lips shut.

Monica's lips quirked minutely, and Lane smiled broadly.

"That's what I said," Lane laughed and then winked at Kierra.

She could feel her face heat. She cleared her throat and then dropped her gaze back to the tablet.

"We'll be staying at an Agency-owned villa on the outskirts of the city center. It has easy access in and out of town if we need a quick getaway. Our local operatives are sweeping it as we speak," Monica reported.

Kierra nodded, "I made a special request for a few bags of the Italian coffee you like before we took off."

"That's our girl," Lane cut in.

"And since it's citrus season, once we land, I'll head to a market and look for those oranges you both loved last summer. Anything else I should have my eye on?"

That was the other perk of being the personal assistant to spies. Kierra was *not* a spy.

pink slip

Every now and then, Monica and Lane brought her to an exotic location so she could make sure that all of their personal needs – even the ones they didn't know they had – were taken care of, while they were out helping to foment a coup or whatever it was that they did. But she was able to experience the adrenaline rush of their missions from a safe remove, either in Command or in a heavily fortified safe house. She only knew as much about the mission as she needed to help Monica and Lane execute their plans. She didn't know any operation particulars. She didn't have high enough security clearance for that. And she didn't want it.

Maybe it was delusional to think this meant that she was safe, but the Peters had never once put her in danger and were adamant that she be protected at all costs. They regularly had her car and home swept for bugs. She had a security detail whenever she traveled out of state without them. And if things had ever gone haywire on a mission, Protocol SG directed that she be promptly moved into their home until her safety could be guaranteed. Unfortunately, that had never happened, but Kierra appreciated the sentiment.

So for the second time today, Monica surprised her.

"We need you in the field."

Kierra laughed, her eyes jumping from Monica's to Lane's and back, waiting for the punchline. But Monica didn't make jokes. And Lane wasn't laughing.

"You've gotta be shitting me," Kierra blurted.

***

Okay, one drawback to traveling in a luxury jet across the Atlantic was that there was nowhere for Kierra to run and hide.

Sure, the jet had a private master suite at the tail, but she was still on a plane. She couldn't stomp out of the office, hop in her car and drive in circles for an hour to clear her head. So, she'd stomped, in her very sexy heels - which Monica hadn't even had the decency to notice, by the way – and laid on the bed, closed her eyes and taken deep breaths, trying to calm her pounding heart.

When that didn't work, she wrenched open the door and walked back to her seat. Monica and Lane stopped talking when she was near and eyed her. She eyed them back, grabbed her cellphone from the small table in front of them, and then stormed back to the bedroom. She connected to the plane's Wi-Fi and sent Maya a message.

Problem. Help.

It took less than thirty seconds for Maya to respond. She was always on her phone or computer, a fact that usually annoyed Kierra, but in moments like this she thought it was a lifesaver.

Listening.

Kierra had to be very particular about what she typed so as not to violate her NDA, potentially compromise the mission (even with the plane's encryption) or betray her own feelings. And it was most tricky not to do the latter. She had been able to survive her crush on Monica and Lane for three years by keeping her work and personal lives separate. She didn't talk about work anymore than was necessary and she certainly didn't talk about her bosses in any great detail.

So Maya's response was just one more shock to add to a day with a new surprise around every corner.

Which boss are you jonesing to fuck today?

Kierra sat up straight and her mouth fell open.

WTF?

pink slip

Maya's text was an immediate and scathing, but loving, read:

> Was that supposed to be a secret? It wasn't.

Kierra frowned and then answered.

> I can't talk about this right now. Never mind.

Maya responded with a string of sad face emojis and then a happy cry emoji.

> Sorry that last one was a typo.
> I'm here to talk whenever. No judgment girl.
> Fuck your bosses, if that's what'll make you happy.
> Just protect yourself.
> Your vagina and your heart.

Kierra wanted to laugh and cry all at the same time. Maya really did give the best advice and usually in the dirtiest way. She sent a heart emoji back in reply and said goodbye. And then she laid back on the bed as confused as before.

Monica was kind enough to give her a full ten minutes to herself before she knocked on the door.

Kierra knew it was Monica, because if it had been Lane, he'd have accompanied his knock with a suggestive query wondering if she was decent or clothed. Monica knocked and then stood in silence. And when Kierra wrenched open the tiny door, she was standing there, straight-backed, her thick, glossy hair hanging just past her shoulders, beautiful light brown face bare of any makeup, in tight black jeans and practical combat boots. She was taller than Kierra by a few inches and so her tits had the gall to be directly at Kierra's eye level, high and prominent in her sensible V-neck t-shirt.

Kierra wanted to be mad at her. She wanted to not want to run her hands over Monica's hips or slip her tongue into her mouth or beg her to do whatever she wanted with her body. But that wasn't who Kierra was.

"Why me?" Kierra asked the question in a hard tone that didn't betray any of her inconvenient lust.

Monica's almost dark eyes were boring into Kierra's as she looked down her nose at her assistant in a way that managed to be sexually suggestive rather than judgmental. She raised one eyebrow, and then slowly lowered it. Kierra felt a small sense of triumph in the knowledge that it only took three years for her to finally ask a question that Monica would have to answer.

Monica moved to the side and gestured down the aisle, silently asking Kierra to return to her seat.

Kierra sighed dramatically and moved past her. Luxury jet aside, the aisle was narrow and even if Kierra had tried to avoid it, some part of her body would still have bumped into Monica's front. But Kierra didn't try to avoid Monica, so her left arm and hip rubbed slowly along her body. Kierra's lips parted in ecstasy and she could have sworn that she heard Monica gasp softly, but it also could have been a figment of her imagination.

Kierra licked her lips and plopped down in her seat with a frown on her face.

Lane leaned forward and grasped her chin between two fingers. "Don't worry, sweet girl. We'd never let anything happen to you."

She almost asked him what he was talking about, because she'd momentarily forgotten that they wanted her to pretend to be a spy. The feel of brushing past Monica and Lane's hand so near to her mouth and the way he always called her sweet girl had sent her head spinning.

It was too much. And yet not nearly enough.

But then she remembered, and she scowled at him.

Lane just laughed and released her face.

"Explain," Kierra said.

Monica tapped at her tablet and then handed it to Kierra.

pink slip

She read the website for a Club Ménage. "Inventive," she said with a roll of her eyes.

"But accurate," Monica responded, her voice all business. "To get in this club you have to be in a ménage, a couple looking for a third or a single person willing to join a pair."

"I'm sure you see our dilemma," Lane said, his head tilted down as he looked at Kierra through his long, light brown eyelashes.

She rolled her eyes at him, hating that he seemed to know how much she loved it when he looked at her that way. "Why not take another agent in with you?"

"We thought of that," Monica acquiesced. "But we don't always work well with others."

"Trust issues," Lane offered.

"We need someone inside who will shore up our cover, maybe do some light surveillance-"

"And who we trust implicitly," Lane finished.

Kierra wanted to be angry again. She wanted to tell them 'hell no' and stomp off back to the bedroom. But she wouldn't. And they knew it. Because they trusted her. And she trusted them. Even though they were spies asking her to purposely put herself in danger.

She shouldn't trust them. She knew that. She was 90% certain that Peters was not their real last name and Monica and Lane were also up in the air as their real first names. But feelings were complicated.

She trusted that they wouldn't have asked her to come into the field with them if they had any other options. She trusted that they would do their best to keep her out of harm's way. And at the end of the day, she trusted herself enough to acknowledge that she was half in love with them and had been for years.

"This is my last week," she whispered.

Monica's back seemed to stiffen.

"We know. And whatever state the mission is in, we'll send you home after your last work date. We promise," Lane said, in a voice that Kierra thought sounded somber. But she quickly decided that that was just her heart playing tricks on her brain.

"I'm not carrying any weapons," Kierra declared.

"That was never an option," Monica replied. "We'll protect you."

"I want a bonus," she added grumpily. "A big one."

Monica nodded; a smile barely visible on her lips.

Lane laughed. "We'll give you anything you want, sweet girl. Anything."

Kierra refused to soften the glare on her face and betray how her stomach flipped at the way he said "anything".

This was absolutely not how she'd planned for her final week of work to go. But a small part of her brain was actually shocked that it had taken three years for her pussy to get her to do something really stupid.

four

Kierra was a professional and she took her job seriously. Even though she was pissed and had refused to speak to Monica or Lane for the rest of the flight, she still performed all her duties to her bosses' exacting standards. She made sure their inflight meals were to their liking. She handled their (forged) paperwork at customs, giving the customs agent her flirtiest smile while he ogled her body and not their paperwork. And she directed their chauffeur in carefully loading their bags into the car.

When they arrived at their safe house, she walked around the villa, making sure that it met their personal specifications, while Monica and Lane trailed behind her, making sure that everything was to their espionage needs. She was frustrated by their constant closeness when just a few hours before she'd have craved it like air. Since she wouldn't be able to see to the needs of their temporary home while they were all out in the field, she gave the cook and maid large pay raises – maybe larger than necessary, but they could afford it – for picking up the slack.

Once the house was in order, Kierra tried to excuse herself from their presence to take a nap in her bedroom. It was frustratingly located in the same wing of the large villa as Monica and Lane's room and their weapons cache.

But Monica stopped her. "Let's have a quick debrief first," she said, not bothering to even pretend as if Kierra had a choice in the matter.

Kierra huffed out a frustrated breath and followed Monica to the office at the end of the short hallway that filled out this wing of the house. There, she found Lane lounging in a plush leather chair at a table.

He smiled and rose, pulling the chair next to him out for her to use. She rolled her eyes and plopped down into it. He laughed as he always did, clearly enjoying her well-deserved tantrum. "Don't be mad at us, sweet girl," he whispered into her ear.

She was too tired to stop the shiver that ran down her spine. She took shallow breaths – into her mouth and slowly out of her nose – and tried to calm herself.

Lane walked around the table and pulled out a chair directly across from Kierra. She tried not to lick her lips as she watched Monica elegantly lower herself into it. Lane didn't sit. Instead, he did that thing that he knew Kierra loved. He stood behind Monica's chair as if he were her sentry, with that easy smile on his face. She wasn't sure how he'd always known exactly the kind of tableau that just did it for her. But he did.

She shifted in her chair, trying to surreptitiously rub her thighs together to ease her ever-present arousal as she thought about all the reasons she had to be mad at them. But then Monica steepled her fingers and her eyes bored into Kierra's and she'd had enough.

"Can we get on with this?" Her voice was irritated, but her mouth had gone dry with lust.

Lane smirked at her, which could mean that he knew exactly what she was going through or he just wanted to unsettle her.

Kierra sighed; it was probably both.

Are you scared?" Monica's voice was serious but soft, which was rare.

"No." She refused to look Monica in the eyes.

"It's okay if you're scared."

She nodded once. It wasn't an admission per se, but Monica took it as one.

"You're not an agent," Monica said.

"No shit."

"Which means that the primary mission objective is to keep you safe."

"And the secondary mission objective?"

"I can't tell you that."

She rolled her eyes. "Because I don't have clearance?"

"Yes."

She locked eyes with Monica finally. "Will I be in danger?" She studied her face, looking for any of the tics she'd become accustomed to as indications of Monica's deception.

Monica's forehead wrinkled as she considered Kierra's question. Or more precisely, as she considered how to answer it. "I want to tell you that you have nothing to worry about, but I don't want to give you a false sense of security. I'd rather you be more cautious than careless."

Kierra was oddly comforted that she didn't detect any deception on Monica's face, at least not any that she recognized. "What exactly do I have to do?" She hated how her voice seemed to shrink as she asked the question, but she couldn't help it. She didn't want to be scared, but this was not her job. Getting coffee and light filing and wandering around open air markets to buy her bosses fruit while they were on assignments, those were in her remit. Not... whatever they were going to ask her to do. At least she didn't think it was. But then Lane leaned forward, his thumbs skimming down Monica's bare arms.

Kierra wondered if they could see her nipples, suddenly hard and at attention, as her eyes tracked that tiny bit of contact.

"We'll only need your help at night," Lane said as he placed a kiss at Monica's hairline.

Kierra pressed her lips together and tried to breath evenly through her nose.

"We'll go to Banovíc's favorite clubs, do a tiny bit of recon and, if we happen to get on his radar, we'll make contact."

"How will we get on his radar?" Kierra asked in a tight whisper. She had an idea; a fantasy.

"That's the easy part," Lane said. "Banovíc likes his sex, the more the merrier. We just have to convince him that whatever we three have going on, he might have a chance to join."

Kierra gulped loudly. "What we three have going on," she said in a dreamlike whisper.

"You, Monica and me," he said, whispering the words straight into Monica's ear.

She wasn't sure what she said in response but to her own ears it sounded pathetic; a guttural moan full of three years of pent up longing.

Kierra excused herself to her bedroom immediately. She could have sworn she heard Lane's laughter following her down the hall. And it was still ringing in her ears when she locked the door, stripped off her clothes and fell face first onto the bed. She shoved her hand into her underwear and rubbed fast circles over her clit, coming immediately before passing out. Not an atypical end to one of her workdays.

When she woke up, it was dusk. It took a moment for her eyes to adjust to the darkened room and for her to remember why this room was not *her* room.

She wasn't surprised to find that her anger at her bosses had lessened minutely, but she was still fairly pissed as she rooted around in her private bathroom for toiletries. She furiously brushed her teeth and showered, hoping the rest of her anger might wash down the drain with the suds. It was only when she was stepping out of the bathroom, a large, indulgently soft towel wrapped around her body, that she realized she didn't have any clothes or makeup. She stomped through her bedroom door, across the hall and into Monica and Lane's room.

Without knocking.

So, it was her fault really, that she interrupted Lane spreading oil over Monica's bare back and ass, his own naked body slightly red, she assumed from the shower.

pink slip

Kierra stood rooted in their sitting room, watching Lane's hands glide over Monica's skin. The bedroom was separated by a small step and alcove. It gave a beautiful cinematic quality to the entire scene. If this weren't her last week, she felt certain she would have been fired on the spot. But damn would it have been worth it. Or at least she thought firing her would have been their response to their intrusion. Instead, Monica and Lane hardly registered her entrance.

Lane continued smoothing oil over Monica's shoulders. He even leaned down to place a small kiss onto her ear. Monica turned to Kierra with her regular hard stare. "Perfect. You're up. We were afraid we were going to have to wake you."

Kierra began to stammer her apologies for rudely barging into their private space. Although, she didn't avert her eyes, so that might have lessened the impact of her amends.

In any case, Monica and Lane didn't seem to care and cut her off mid-sentence. "We need to get you dressed for tonight."

"That's," Kierra gulped, her eyes locking onto the way the tip of Lane's cock was brushing against the curve of Monica's butt. "That's why I came in here. I don't have anything to wear."

"We've handled it," Lane said matter-of-factly.

"Come here," Monica said. Her voice was always hard, everything she said sounded like a barking demand. It was just her nature and Kierra was never perturbed by her tone. Not even now. Because she liked it too much. Kierra took a few tentative steps toward her bosses, her mouth beginning to water as she took in the gradient shades of brown of Monica's breasts and nipples. As Kierra neared, Lane pressed one more kiss to Monica's shoulder and moved away to put on a pair of boxers. Monica extended her hand to Kierra, who grasped it, shocked at how much she'd longed to touch Monica in this way, in any way, over the past three years.

Monica rose and pulled Kierra to the walk-in closet. Kierra turned her head to see Lane following.

Inside the closet, Kierra could see why it was easier to not have her pack; she didn't own anything that would have fit the dress code for this trip. Almost every stitch of clothing in the closet was mesh or soft leather or flowing, thin silk, and barely enough fabric to cover their bodies. She guessed it made sense. Where they were going, the whole point was to see and be seen.

"I was thinking you should wear this," Monica said, pulling a slinky jersey dress that Kierra knew would hug every one of her curves. It was a simple but classy deep purple frock that fit Monica's style perfectly. And Monica's style was one of Kierra's areas of expertise since she'd spent every morning for three years trying to fashion outfits that might catch her eye.

"But I was thinking about this," Lane said from behind her. Kierra turned and was not that shocked to see that the garment – a very generous word considering – in his hand was practically see-through.

Kierra squinted at it. Nope, actually it was fully see-through. But it was a beautiful long-sleeved, floor length silk dress with artfully placed floral embroidery that might – might – cover all of Kierra's important bits.

"Which do you prefer?"

Kierra's eyes closed in ecstasy at Monica's whispered words in her ear; her body suddenly so close. If that wasn't the question of the century, or at least the last three years.

She answered honestly, "Both. I like them both."

When she opened her eyes, Lane's smiling face made her want to swoon. "That's our girl." He whispered the words like a prayer.

Monica's breath tickled her ear.

Kierra shivered.

And then Lane disrupted the moment, whatever it was, with a sharp clap of his hands. "I'm going to defer to my wife's expert opinion tonight. Wear the purple one." He raised the dress in his hands and looked at it with mournful eyes before hanging it back on the rack. "But I want to pick her shoes," he said, turning back to them with a playful wiggle of his eyebrows.

"Naturally," Monica breathed, moving away from Kierra.

Kierra hadn't had the most PG dreams before she started working for the Peters. Why should she? She was a young, healthy woman in her twenties. But there was something about lusting after her married bosses that sent her right over the edge and she'd spent the past three years chasing every one of her sexual desires in her fantasies. She thought she'd explored them all, but her imagination had completely failed her because she'd never even considered how absolutely erotic it could be to have Monica and Lane dress her.

Monica threw the slinky purple dress on the bed. She retrieved the oil Lane had been spreading over her own body, poured some into her hands and then began to spread it up one arm and down the other. Monica moved her hands over Kierra's shoulders, her thumbs grazing her collar bone.

The rational part of Kierra's brain wanted to interrupt and remind Kierra that she could moisturize her own body. but the not rational part of her brain made her bite her bottom lip and told her to shut the fuck up and enjoy this, it might never happen again.

"May I?" Monica gestured toward the towel wrapped around Kierra's body.

Kierra nodded.

Monica delicately – more delicately than Kierra had ever seen her do anything – pulled the two sides of the towel apart to expose her naked body, almost as if she was revealing a treat for herself.

Kierra's skin flushed under Monica's gaze, goosebumps rising all over her body, her nipples hardening. How many times had she dreamed about Monica looking at her naked body exactly like this, as if she was good enough to eat?

Monica pressed her hands flat to Kierra's sternum; a soft, reassuring pressure. "You know we'd never let anything happen to you, right?"

Kierra's eyes widened at Monica's whisper. That soft voice from earlier stroking her, but this time also pleading. Kierra felt foolish thinking it, but her voice almost sounded loving.

She raised her eyes to lock with Monica's. "I-" But her words were cut off as Monica's hands moved down her chest, cupping her breasts, her thumbs moving gently over her nipples.

Kierra sucked in a harsh breath.

Monica's hands continued down her torso as she spoke. "You're the best assistant we've ever had. I know I don't tell you often enough, but we couldn't have managed the last three years without you." Monica wrapped her arms around Kierra and pulled her naked body to hers. She moved her hands up her back, locking her in place. "We're going to miss you," she whispered, her breath tickling Kierra's lips.

Kierra wasn't sure if Monica had ever said so many words to her at once. But she knew that she'd never said anything to her so gently, and it threatened to break something inside of her. Her resolve, surely, but something else, something buried deep in her heart; something like hope. But she couldn't let that happen. There was a pile of words balancing on the tip of her tongue, but she could only whisper, "I can't stay," even though that wasn't nearly the whole story.

Lane's voice, so close behind her, made Kierra jump. "We know, sweet girl. Doesn't mean we're not sad about it."

Monica kept Kierra's body pressed to hers as Lane leaned down to rub oil onto her legs. His hands never strayed anywhere they shouldn't, although if their spy outfit had an HR manager, Kierra was sure they'd say that all of this was inappropriate. And they'd be right, of course. But as it was, Kierra was the entire administrative staff and, as acting but unofficial HR manager, she kept her lips shut tight as Lane oiled her body and Monica's deadly serious stare pinned her in place, their breasts pressed together and their breath mingling.

When Kierra's skin was glossy from the oil, which smelled slightly of lavender, Monica finally released her with a barely perceptible frown. She and Lane wiped their hands on Kierra's towel and then Monica picked up her dress. Kierra reached for it and Lane grabbed her hand, pressing his body against her back.

Kierra couldn't help the strangled cry that escaped her lips.

"Let us do that, sweet girl," he whispered against her cheek.

Monica leaned forward and Kierra lifted one foot and then the other into the neck of the dress. She tried to keep her entire body from shaking as they pulled it over her hips and torso, smoothing the fabric against her skin. Kierra slipped her arms into the short Bardot sleeves. Lane's hands circled her neck gently, his thumbs massaging her at the top of her spine, while Monica scraped her nails softly across Kierra's covered nipples.

Kierra moaned. She had only so much willpower.

"Now for your equipment," Lane said, his voice full of glee.

Kierra squinted her eyes in confusion, her brain clouded by lust. Monica turned to grab a small box from the bed that Kierra had been too distracted to notice. She opened it. Kierra recognized equipment she'd ordered and sent for repair but had never had cause to use.

"This ear bud is directly linked to ones we'll be wearing," Monica said, pointing at the item with her pinky. "You'll swallow this temporary tracker. We don't plan on letting you out of our sight, but if we get separated, we'll be able to find you."

Kierra nodded and reached for the earbud. Monica helped her situate it comfortably. Lane moved away and when Kierra grabbed the tracker, he handed her a glass of water.

"It's biodegradable. It'll disappear in twelve hours," he informed her.

She nodded again.

"Now. Are we ready to have some fun?"

Kierra shivered. Weren't they already?

five

Kierra didn't know what European sex clubs were supposed to look like, but Club Ménage felt very uninspired; like a bad porno or a 70's spy movie. She said as much to Monica and Lane. They both smiled indulgently at her and then turned back to scanning the room.

Kierra had never really given much thought to what missions were like, but she'd just assumed that it was nonstop action. If asked, she would have guessed there were guns blazing, Monica throwing off her heels to run barefoot down a deserted street after a hitman, Lane scaling rooftops to catch a rogue operative. You know, like in the movies. So she was very disappointed to find that this mission, the first and likely only mission she'd ever be on, was boring as all get out.

She looked out over the room with disgust. There were tall tables at the center where people dressed as if at a fancy cocktail party – *not* a European sex club – stood, talking and drinking. She, Monica and Lane were sitting on a very cliché tufted couch, wide enough for them to invite a few friends and long enough for them to recline if they wanted or needed.

Kierra slouched against Lane's side.

"What's the matter, sweet girl?" he asked, but kept his eyes on the crowd in front of them.

"I'm bored," Kierra sighed.

Monica turned toward her; eyebrows raised. "I thought you were worried we were putting you in harm's way. Now you're bored?"

"I'm not saying I want a shootout to start, but this is a sex club, is it not?" Kierra whispered back.

Kierra was a master of decoding Monica's expressions. And by the small quirk of her almost smile, she knew that she was amused, but she turned away to scan the crowd before the smile had time to fully bloom on her beautiful face. Lane's pleasure was much less difficult to decipher. His rumble of laughter bounced her body along his chest. For the past three years, Monica's vague amusement and Lane's joyful laugh had been enough, more than enough, to make Kierra's day. But that was before she'd had their hands all over her body.

Kierra leaned forward to rest her chin on Monica's bare shoulder, which gave her a very nice view down the plunging neckline of her dress.

"You promised me fun," she said in a soft whisper.

"Lane," Monica stressed, "promised you fun. I'm working."

Kierra, feeling bold and horny, raised her head, pressed her lips to Monica's ear and moaned. "It wouldn't be fun without you."

Kierra felt Monica's body tense and she turned to stare at her. Their mouths were so close. Kierra knew that Monica could see her pleading for a kiss with her eyes. And she looked as if she was just about to give her exactly what she wanted – had wanted for three years – when Lane leaned forward.

"He's here," he whispered. Monica's eyes sobered and she turned back to the crowd.

Kierra tried not to pout, even though she wanted to. This was serious business. She leaned forward and grasped her glass of wine, raising it to her mouth, barely wetting her lips as her eyes scanned the crowd.

She spotted President Banović easily. Honestly, she would have been disappointed if a bona fide eastern European dictator dared to enter a sex club under the radar. What would be the point of being a supreme ruler if you had to slink into a bordello to get your rocks off?

He was wearing a clearly expensive, but very ill-fitting designer military uniform, even though he'd never once served in his country's military or any other.

"What is it with dictators and terrible fashion?"

Lane chuckled. "Very good question," he said and placed a soft kiss to her shoulder.

"I count three on his personal guard," he whispered into Kierra's skin loud enough for Monica to hear.

"There are two more in the crowd at your two and ten," Monica replied.

Kierra leaned forward to place her glass on the table in front of them, surreptitiously glancing around the room, clocking all of Banovíc's guards.

Monica ran a hand down Kierra's back and Lane gripped her hip tightly.

When she straightened, Monica turned toward her and leaned forward. Kierra couldn't stop her heart racing, thinking it was finally happening. And as if Monica knew that, she smirked, like a real, visible, Kierra could have seen it from the moon, smirk. In comparison to her regular micro-expressions, that not subtle movement of her lips felt like a grand gesture. Monica raised an eyebrow, that smirk mocking her, and then she reached out to grasp the side of Lane's head. Their lips crushed together right in front of Kierra's face. She was momentarily dejected, but then she saw the flash of their tongues swirling together and her sex clenched in lustful glee.

Out of the corner of her eye she saw Banovíc settle into a couch a few feet away and notice them.

"He's looking over here," she whispered to Monica and Lane.

They stopped kissing but kept their mouths close. "Of course he is," Lane said, "I've got the two most beautiful women in the room with me."

Kierra giggled.

Monica turned toward her, moving her hand from Lane's face to the space between Kierra's breasts. From far away, it would look like Monica was whispering seductive words to her. "Keep him in your peripheral vision. Don't be obvious. Tonight is purely for recon." Monica's index finger circled one of Kierra's nipples and she gasped. "There's absolutely no need to rush."

They weren't the most romantic of words, but Kierra felt very seduced, nonetheless.

***

They spent the next hour or so pretending to slowly sip their drinks while surveying the other groupings around the room. There seemed to be a ménage for every flavor but Banovíc's eyes kept returning to them. Eventually they pretended to finally notice and turned to acknowledge his attentions with raised glasses, but nothing more.

After a while, more people moved to the couches and Kierra's eyes bulged as miles and miles of flesh was bared to the slightly cool air of the room and her greedy attention; some she was happy to see, some she wasn't. She tried to keep her eyes moving, so that she could keep track of Banovíc's guards. Every now and then she'd get distracted by Lane's hand on her hip or Monica's on her thigh. But in all Kierra thought she'd done a passable job on her first mission, since she was a poet, not a spy.

Monica turned toward her after they'd been at the club for around two hours. "Ready to go home?"

Kierra nodded, only in that moment feeling the coming exhaustion of jet lag and stress threatening to descend upon her. They stood to leave but were cut off by one of Banovíc's guards, one who Lane had guessed was his most trusted since he hadn't left the president's side once all night. Until now.

He stepped in front of them and Lane's hand tensed on Kierra's hip. Monica reached down and twined her fingers with Kierra's. When the guard spoke, his very accented English was a mean, guttural hiss that made Kierra's pulse race in fear. "We would like to invite you for a drink," he said to Lane.

Lane craned his head to look at Banovíc and nodded. "Unfortunately, we were just leaving. Maybe next time."

The guard seemed frustrated. He turned and looked at his boss. Whatever silent thing passed between them was settled and he turned back to them. "Very well. My employer is having a private party here in one week. Please leave your name at reception and we will send an invitation."

"Sounds like a plan," Lane said amiably. Monica and Kierra turned to Banovíc and smiled, which seemed to please him. And then they were on their way.

When they were safe in the villa, Kierra finally let her body relax and yawned loudly. Monica grasped her hand and led her to their wing of the house. At Kierra's door, she turned and reached up to Kierra's ear, pulling the earbud loose. And then it happened. Monica leaned down and pressed her lips to Kierra's. It was chaste and teasing and perfect. Kierra wanted more, but she was too tired to ask for it.

"You did well, sweet girl," Monica whispered against her lips and then let her go.

Lane cradled Kierra's head gently and pressed his mouth to hers. "Sleep well."

Kierra watched them enter their bedroom before she pushed into her own.

She could hardly tear her dress off fast enough. She slipped into bed and masturbated to the mental image of Lane and Monica. The only difference this time was that she didn't have to wonder what their hands and mouths would feel like against her skin.

Her orgasm was intense and left her a sweaty, shivering mess, naked on top of her sheets. She couldn't stop herself from screaming their names. She hoped they heard.

Lane

Lane intrinsically knew that a large portion of good spy work meant being seen when necessary so that you could go unseen at other times. It was part of the reason working with Monica had always been so easy. When they wanted to be noticed, Lane could pull attention with his loud mouth whenever necessary. It never took much work; people loved a spectacle. His loud personality also took the pressure off of Monica and allowed her to keep a watchful eye on their surroundings. While everyone had their eyes on Lane, she had her eyes on them.

Now that they'd made first contact with Banović, they needed to make sure to be seen in all the right places for tourists of their caliber, because he would be looking for them. In less than an hour after leaving their cover names at Club Ménage, they'd watched as the Serbian intelligence agency began investigating their identities: entrance into the country, personal websites and banking history. It was a strong cover and they weren't worried about it, but their online footprint was only half of the story.

They began spending time out during the day, casually skirting along the edges of Banović's associates: corrupt politicians and other wealthy, bored socialites interested in kink. They made sure to eat at the right restaurants, shopped in the right stores and eyed the right men and women as they passed. That was the easy part.

The hard part was at night. If he was as interested as he'd seemed their first night at Club Ménage, they knew Banović would be looking for them at the city's other clubs, wanting to confirm for himself that their tastes were compatible with his. They were not, but Lane's easy smile always fooled people into accepting him as a kindred spirit. The problem was that, to convince Banović that they were potential playmates, they would have to put Kierra in his line of sight, and they agreed that the goal was to do that as little as possible.

After Club Ménage, they'd visited a few of Banovíc's haunts around the city without Kierra. They never stayed for long, they just needed him to see them. And on this mission Monica's bored gaze fit their cover perfectly. Why would she want anyone else, when Kierra was (safe) at their villa? It seemed to be working. Every time Banovíc saw them out without Kierra, he seemed to grow more interested in them and in her absence.

Lane pulled out a chair for Monica at the city's best French restaurant, Ver de Terre. One thing they did actually have in common with Banovíc was that they also hated French food. He'd never visited this restaurant, no matter how many invitations the head chef extended with the promise that he was certain Banovíc would love his version of French cuisine. It hadn't worked so far, but the chef had made sure to host as many of Banovíc's political allies and personal playthings, hoping to curry the dictator's favor. But this lunch wasn't about Banovíc. It was about his second in command.

Martin Stepanov was Banovíc's oldest political ally and just as corrupt as his boss. Their mission directives were limited to dealing with Banovíc, but he and Monica were nothing if not cautious. And in their experience, it was always prudent to explore the complicated web of power and relationships and give some consideration to the consequences that a power vacuum might create. Reliable intel indicated that Stepanov was the most likely candidate to seize power should Banovíc be removed.

But there was less information on Stepanov than either Lane or Monica liked. He enjoyed staying in Banovíc's shadow and that made them both uncomfortable. The only kinds of people who enjoy being second in command are people too weak to lead or who prefer to do their dirt in private. Lane and Monica agreed that at best Stepanov would be neutralized without Banović and at worst he could become even more dangerous than his predecessor. It was in their best interest to decipher which path he might take before they completed their mission.

As far as Lane and Monica were concerned, all the intel in the world was nothing until they got the chance to look Stepanov directly in the eyes to see exactly what kind of man he was. So they leaned back amiably in their chairs, the sunlight spilling into Ver de Terre's dining room, shopping bags full of frivolous and overpriced luxury trinkets in the free chairs at their table as if the contents cost nothing. And they waited.

They'd been seated at their table for five minutes, chatting, scanning the menu, looking out at the street and pretending to drink glasses of wine when they noticed the maître d' walking quietly between the tables surrounding them, apologizing to the other guests. Lane noticed but didn't flinch. He grabbed a piece of bread on the table, drawing Monica's eyes to him. He watched her realize what was happening. They said nothing. Simply observed.

Lane had a gun at his back as usual. Monica was armed with some of her favorite and sharpest knives, hidden artfully all over her body beneath her tight jeans and soft cashmere sweater. She crossed her right leg over her left. Someone watching them would think that she did so to lean closer to him, which she did, and gave him one of her prettiest smiles as she shifted her body so that she had better access to the knife sheathed in her knee-high boot.

Her smile was genuine and for a second it distracted Lane, as always. Which was not good.

"Don't smile at me like that on a mission," he whispered.

"Why, old man?"

He popped a piece of bread in his mouth and watched the maître d' moving in his peripheral vision. "I might be an old man the way you've been riding me every night of this trip.

I'm probably one good fuck away from a heart attack." He smiled innocently at her.

She bit her bottom lip and batted her eyes at him. And then she whispered, "They're clearing out the dining room."

Lane's smile didn't falter, he just smiled at her, one slow blink his only acknowledgement of what she'd said.

"You gonna keep taking all of your frustrations out of me?" He asked, leaning into her. "Or are you going to finally let Kierra know how riled up you get when she crosses something off your to-do list?"

He wasn't sure if Monica was going to answer, but he noted her small exhale of relief when the maître d' stopped at their table. Lane was ready for him to tell them to leave as he watched a group of angry diners shuffle out of the restaurant behind him.

"Are you ready to order?" he asked instead.

One of Lane's eyebrows quirked up in response. "What would you recommend?"

As he began to answer, a small entourage entered the restaurant. The maître d' hid it well, but he jumped when his eyes landed on Stepanov. He turned back to Monica and Lane, bowed slightly in a deferential manner that Lane assumed the very rich and powerful in Serbia preferred, and then motioned for another waiter to serve them. "I am sorry. I must go greet another important guest, but please enjoy."

Lane and Monica didn't listen to the waiter and so they weren't entirely sure what they ordered. They just needed to get the man out of their line of vision quickly.

Monica tapped her left index finger on the table four times, one for each guard stationed in plain sight inside the restaurant. Lane pretended to take a sip of wine and informed her of the car idling out on the street and another car with two bodyguards across from it.

"That's a lot of manpower for a casual lunch," Monica breathed as she reached up to smooth the collar of Lane's already immaculate suit jacket.

He turned his head to brush his lips along her hand. He looked at her with all the love he felt. "Either he's paranoid or our cover is blown."

She bit her lip seductively, trailed her hand down his chest and around his waist, lowered her eyelashes and nodded.

The sound of a man clearing his throat interrupted them. When they turned, one of Stepanov's guards stood in front of their table waiting patiently. Lane's hand rested high on Monica's calf, his fingers gripping the handle of the knife in her boot. Her hand rested on the hilt of his gun. They waited.

"Hello," the guard said in heavily accented English. "Please accept this small token on behalf of my employer."

Their waiter moved forward, placed a bucket of ice with a bottle of very expensive champagne on the table. He lifted the bottle from the ice and showed its label to Lane, who nodded as he read the vintage. Lane tilted his head to nod again across the dining room at Stepanov.

Martin Stepanov was like Banović in many ways. They were of similar, average height and balding, with a clear penchant for expensive clothing. However, instead of Banović's fake military uniform, Stepanov enjoyed very expensive tailored suits that almost made him look like a legitimate businessman and not a money launderer. He was sitting next to an attractive younger man who intel indicated was his lover, masquerading as his private secretary. The waiter opened the champagne and poured Monica and Lane a glass each. They held them up to respectfully salute Stepanov and took long sips.

Stepanov smiled widely to indicate his approval and then nodded to the guard. Lane's hand tightened on Monica's knife.

The guard reached into his jacket pocket and pulled out a piece of paper. An address was printed on the piece of thick, beautiful card stock.

pink slip

"My employer has heard good things of you from our Esteemed President. He would like to invite you to a private party that he is having tonight at this address."

Lane smiled his big, bright, Texas oil baron smile and raised his glass again to Stepanov. "It would be our pleasure, wouldn't it, sweetheart?"

Monica smiled pleasantly, "Absolutely."

"Wonderful," the guard replied, the smile on his face looking genuine, which made the hairs on the back of Lane's neck stand up, but he wasn't yet sure why. "I will convey your acceptance." He turned to walk away and then stopped, turning back to their table. "I am told that you have another. Please know that the invitation extends to her as well. Per the particular request of our Esteemed President."

Lane and Monica's smiles didn't falter.

"She'll consider that an honor," Monica said, her voice light, even though her hand was tightly gripping Lane's gun.

The guard walked back to the table and then, just like that, Stepanov's party rose from their chairs and headed toward the door. Stepanov turned toward them as he walked to the exit to smile his goodbye, his eyes roving over Lane's face in appreciation.

They both wanted to leave, especially Monica. They wanted to get back to the villa and make sure that Kierra was all right. But that would raise every alarm they'd been working to avoid. No one notices the man who politely and quietly robs a bank and then walks away, because they're too busy watching after the guy running in the opposite direction. So they stayed put, pretended to chat about the weather, ate small bites of food that tasted like it was going to give Lane heartburn in a few hours. It was at least half an hour before they stood from their table, thanked the chef and maître d' for their meal, not at all shocked to find that Stepanov had paid their bill.

They didn't speak until they were in their chauffeured car on the way back to their villa.

"Calm down," Lane said in a soothing tone. He gripped the back of Monica's neck and smoothed circles at the tender flesh there.

"We shouldn't have asked her to do this," Monica said. Her body was rigid beside him and her voice was full of worry. "This isn't her job."

"And we won't let anything happen to her."

Monica shirked his hand from her neck and turned toward him, her eyes full of fear. "We should send her home."

Lane took a deep breath. "If you think that's best, we can do that."

"You're agreeing? Just like that."

"If you really want to send her home. We can."

Monica nodded. And then stopped, turning toward the window to watch the city pass them by.

"We were supposed to have this last week with her. Just the three of us in Command. Normal."

Lane smiled and leaned forward to whisper in her ear, "It was never normal, darlin'."

six

What does a personal assistant to spies do in a foreign country while her bosses are off doing the actual spy work? Kierra usually had more notice before a trip and liked to research museums to visit and plays to see. But she also wasn't usually a part of her bosses' operations. Knowing that Banović and his guards knew what she looked like made her nervous, even if the likelihood that she'd run into them on the street seemed very low. But still, in lieu of a meticulously curated sightseeing itinerary, she decided to take an actual break from her job while Monica and Lane were out scaling buildings, hacking security systems or whatever it was they did.

Kierra worked on her poetry collection while lounging by the pool. She took naps in the middle of the day and binge-watched tv shows she'd been too busy to see over the past three years. It was actually quite nice for a while and after a couple of days, she'd almost forgotten why she was even in Serbia. Although this trip's effect on her relationship with her bosses was not so easily forgotten. That was certainly a good thing because Kierra didn't want to forget that at all.

Her bosses' schedules were irregular. They usually all had breakfast together in the dining room down the hall from their bedrooms. Monica and Lane waited until the food had been served and their cook was on the other side of the villa to discuss the mission's progress.

They didn't include Kierra in the conversation unless they needed to delegate some admin work to her. She kept her tablet close and jumped on each task quickly and efficiently. After breakfast they showered, separately, much to Kierra's chagrin, and dressed for the day. Kierra usually slipped on one of the tiny bathing suits she'd found in Monica's well-stocked walk-in closet, while they dressed in sophisticated clothing to keep up their cover as a Texas oil magnate and his spoiled wife.

Just before they left the house, Monica had begun to lean down and press a soft kiss to the side of Kierra's mouth and then Lane would smile that same gleeful smile at her as he reached down to playfully swat her ass in farewell. It was the literal stuff of her actual dreams.

"Call if you need me," Kierra always yelled after them, her heart beating fast in her chest.

They never called, because they never needed her.

Monica and Lane knew that Banovíc had been looking into their cover and so they made themselves as visible as possible. They wandered the city, spending money, eating in all the right restaurants, meeting with all the right socialites. Seeing and being seen. He had apparently been satisfied that they were who they said they were and their invitations to his private engagement had arrived the day after their initial encounter at Club Ménage.

"Mr. & Mrs. Hudson and pet," Kierra had screamed when she saw the address on the envelope. "And. Pet?"

"It's language they use in the subculture," Lane had said in a placating tone. "Calm down."

"And? Pet?" Kierra had screamed again.

She'd been ready to scream some more when Monica grasped the invitation from her hands and threw it haphazardly onto the table. She pulled Kierra's body to hers and ran her hands up and down her bare arms, encouraging Kierra to take deep breaths. Kierra had only then remembered that she was in another of those very skimpy bathing suits and her nipples tightened at Monica's touch.

"Calm down, sweet girl," Lane repeated. "It's our cover."

"I'm not your pet," she said in a fierce whisper aimed at Monica.

Monica's smirk unnerved her, because Kierra knew the question it asked before Lane said it.

"You sure about that?"

pink slip

Whatever witty comeback Kierra normally might have come up with died on her tongue.

She'd been halfway toward an orgasm after they'd left before she realized what she should have said. "You have to ask me to be your pet first."

But besides their increased physical contact, very little had changed. Unfortunately. And after three days cooped up in the villa like a hermit, Kierra's sexual frustration was too much to bear. She threw on a pair of tight jean shorts and her old cropped band t-shirt and headed out to the city center, hoping to walk off her lust.

If she'd been a real spy, she would have let Monica and Lane know where she was going before she left. If she'd been a real spy, she'd have found another temporary tracker and swallowed it. Just in case. But Kierra was not a real spy. And so she only had herself to blame when, while standing in the museum of modern art admiring some abstract floral painting by an artist she'd never heard of and whose name she couldn't pronounce, she spotted one of Banovíc's guards, easily recognizing him from Club Ménage.

He stood sentry to her left, guarding the room. She turned her head minutely and saw that another guard had done the same to her right. She also noted that all the other visitors who had previously been in this room had disappeared. And she was alone. Kierra pursed her lips together and tried not to scream or run, even though she desperately wanted to do both of those things. But she still jumped when she felt Banovíc's finger move her hair aside, grazing her neck, so that he could whisper into her ear.

"Now what is a pretty little bird like you doing out all alone?" His English was much less accented than his guard's. Kierra knew that was probably connected to a student exchange year in the U.S. as a teenager and two years at Wharton for his business degree; all the trappings of a Western-sponsored regime.

She took in a few breaths through her nose and tried to catalogue everything she knew about him, which was a lot since she collated mission intelligence, and found comfort in not being as ignorant as he seemed to presume she was.

She turned to him, affecting a pleasant but dim smile. "I love art," she said, as if that was obvious.

He let that one finger trace along her neck and jaw. Just before it reached her mouth she stepped out of his grasp. He did a passable job of smothering his rage. It was a quick, but intense glow that Kierra only caught because Monica was much better at controlling her emotions.

"I don't know how you treat your pets," she said in a voice that thankfully hid her disgust at the word, "but where I come from, we don't touch other people's property." She leaned forward and whispered just low enough that he was forced to lean in if he wanted to hear, "Unless you ask for permission first."

The lascivious smile that spread across his face made Kierra's skin crawl, but she tamped down on expressing anything that wouldn't serve her in this moment. She smiled at him again, slowly, seductively and then turned on her heels to walk away.

"I look forward to seeing you at my party, little bird," Banovíc called after her.

Kierra didn't acknowledge him. She kept her back straight as she walked out of the museum. Her lips were pressed tight together as she hailed a cab with one hand. On the drive back to the villa, her nails bit into her palms as she fought the urge to scream out her terror. It was only when she was safely inside the foyer that she let out a harsh breath and the tears sprang to her eyes.

"Where the hell have you been?" Lane rounded into the foyer, skin red and splotchy in anger. It was rare that he abandoned the congenial mask that he offered the world or raised his voice above a sedate Southern drawl, which Kierra still wasn't sure was real. In three years, she felt certain that she'd only seen him truly angry once. And that one time paled in comparison to the rage she saw distorting his face now.

"Answer me, Kierra. Where were you?"

She opened her mouth to speak but wailed loudly instead. And then Lane's arms were around her shoulders as he walked her to the living room. He took her to the couch and settled her into Monica's arms. Kierra didn't want to cry in front of them. No one likes crying in front of their bosses. But she'd been so scared and had bottled it up so well. And now that the anxiety she'd felt had broken free she couldn't stop her tears.

Monica's arms encircled her, holding her, smoothing her hair. Kierra could feel Lane's solid presence, oozing with rage, as he paced in front of them.

"Are you hurt?" Monica asked when Kierra's sobs finally began to ease.

She shook her head. Some of the tension radiating from Lane's body seeped away but he kept moving.

"What happened? Tell us everything," Monica said in a soft command that cut through her lingering discomfort.

After she told them about running into Banovíc, Lane's pacing only sped up.

"He was following me," Kierra said.

Lane shot her a sardonic look. "Of course he was. We've been talking about that for days."

Kierra's face heated. She felt foolish. In her frustration, she'd behaved as if she were still just her spy bosses' anonymous PA, not their pet and an integral part of their cover. She'd assumed when they were talking about Banovíc having them followed they meant Monica and Lane. She hadn't thought Banovíc thought of her as more than a pretty bauble on their arms. But she could see now that was exactly the point.

"He wants to fuck me," she blurted out.

Lane gave her another withering look. "Of course he does. Have you looked in a mirror?"

Kierra bit her bottom lip, trying desperately not to be so pleased with the compliment, even if he offered it to her in an annoyed tone.

"Did you feel threatened?" Monica asked the question while continuing to smooth Kierra's hair. Kierra tried not to acknowledge to herself the irony of Monica petting her or that she was basically preening under the attention. She simply pressed her body even more firmly into Monica's side.

"Not like 'our cover is blown' threatened. Just in a 'that guy gives me rapey vibes' kind of way."

"Okay," Lane said, "that's good. Well, not good. That guy gives me rapey vibes as well. But our cover's probably still intact and I don't plan on letting him get near either one of you alone again."

"I can take care of myself," Monica replied drily.

Lane smiled at her, his first smile since Kierra had arrived back at the villa. But then he looked at her with a serious scowl. "Next time you want to leave here without us you arrange a guard, swallow a tracker and let us know. You hear?"

"Yes, sir," she said and then bit her lip.

The stare he gave her back was stern, but not in an angry way.

Kierra pressed her face more firmly into the crook of Monica's neck, inhaling the spicy scent of her cologne, and finally let herself relax now that she was well and truly safe.

***

After the afternoon's excitement, Kierra would have liked to hang around the villa, eat ice cream and let Monica pet her until she fell asleep.

But there was a party happening at one of the city's most popular fetish clubs that Banovíc liked to frequent. There were a lot of sex clubs in this moderately sized Eastern European city, which seemed strange to Kierra, but when in

pink slip

Novi Sad, she guessed. Kierra had considered protesting, willing to make the case that since this club wasn't ménage specific, they technically didn't need her. But then Lane had shown her the dress they'd picked out for her, a short mesh, sleeveless thing that wouldn't even begin to cover her important bits. And then he'd oiled her body, while Monica stepped into a white midi slip dress that seemed to flow over her body like water when she walked. and Kierra had gotten distracted by the barest flash of her areolas. And then she'd been shimmying into a flesh-toned thong, but no bra, trying not to get her nails stuck in the mesh of her dress. And before she knew it Lane was walking ahead of them in his casual slate gray business suit as if he was going to a business meeting. He opened the door to the club whose name Kierra couldn't pronounce but intel translated as Peep, and Monica was grasping her hand, leading her inside.

If the problem with Club Ménage was that there wasn't enough action, the problem with Peep, in Kierra's opinion, was that there was too much. One second, they were outside on a quiet, out of the way street and the next second, they were in the middle of what felt like one big writhing mess.

Kierra wasn't sure if Monica had been to this club before or if she'd studied its layout closely, but she deftly moved them through the very public orgy happening basically at the club's entrance, up a flight of stairs and into a tamer sitting area. The music wasn't so loud up there, and the setup was fairly like Ménage with big plush couches along the perimeter. Kierra guessed if you've seen one Eastern European sex club, then you've seen them all, and sighed at the lack of imagination.

The only thing of real interest, and she guessed part of the reason why the club was called Peep, was that in the middle of the floor there was a clear Plexiglas circle. As they walked over it, Kierra looked down and got a bird's eye view of downstairs' orgy. She decided that from this vantage point it was much more palatable. She then noticed that all the club's walls had Plexiglas windows into other rooms so people could witness the events around them. She nodded absently, giving the club points for interest.

Monica and Lane moved across the sitting area and took possession of a small loveseat in the corner. Their perch had a clear view of the stairs and a door in the opposite corner, which led to Kierra didn't know where.

Lane reached to pull Kierra into his lap.

"There are other, bigger couches over there," she protested, not sure if sitting in Lane's lap was the best way for them to stay on task. Well, it certainly wasn't the best way for her to stay on task, but they were professionals.

"This seat has the best view for our operation. Now sit," Monica demanded, patting Lane's lap.

Lane quirked his eyebrow at Kierra, leaned back into the couch and put one arm over the side and one along the back behind Monica.

Kierra lowered herself gingerly onto his legs, trying not to think about all the dreams she'd had that started just like this.

She tried not to squirm, which only made her squirm even more. She shouldn't have been shocked when she felt Lane's dick begin to harden beneath her, but she was. She turned to him with wide eyes.

"What'd you expect? Stop moving and he'll settle down."

Monica scoffed, "What'd I tell you about talking about your cock like it's a person?"

Lane leaned over and kissed Monica's cheek. "It's big enough to be."

Kierra giggled. Monica shook her head but turned to kiss him back warmly.

Just then they were interrupted by a waitress. She smiled and nodded while placing a bucket of champagne and glasses in front of them. And then she turned to nod across the room.

Kierra recognized the man staring back at them in his crisp business suit as Martin Stepanov, Banović's finance minister. He raised his glass and they all nodded as the waitress opened the champagne bottle and poured them each a glass.

"Is this a good thing?" Kierra asked, using her champagne flute to hide her mouth.

"Too early to tell," Monica replied, with a smile on her face as she ran a hand up Kierra's thigh.

Kierra couldn't blame her response on the champagne, since she hadn't drunk any. And she couldn't blame it on this afternoon's run-in with the European dictator they were gathering intel on. But she could blame the days, months, three years' worth of pent up lust for her bosses for making her moan as Monica's cool hand, slightly wet from her champagne flute, made contact with her skin. She moved her legs slightly apart, the invitation clear.

Monica's hand didn't move higher, but she didn't take it away either. She did lean forward and swipe her tongue across Kierra's nipple, through the mesh of her dress. She kept her eyes on Kierra's face the whole time.

Lane's hips shifted beneath her and Kierra's head fell back in ecstasy as Monica began to suckle on her nipple, her wet mouth applying the perfect amount of pressure. Kierra's legs fell open obscenely and she began to thrust her hips forward, her body begging Monica to touch her more, everywhere.

Monica dragged her tongue up Kierra's chest and her neck. And then they were face-to-face. "This isn't the mission, Kierra. We can just watch."

"Just tell us to stop and it's done," Lane added.

Kierra wanted to laugh, like really laugh at the absurdity of their words. Who cares about the fucking mission? She sure as hell didn't. She kept her gaze level with Monica's and her voice serious. "You're supposed to be the best spies in the world. If you don't know that I wanted you before this mission, I'm going to have to question your credentials."

Kierra's eyes widened as a not-small smile spread across Monica's lips. She'd never seen a full-fledged smile from her before. She wanted to bottle it and keep it with her forever. But then Kierra's mouth fell open in a groan as Monica's hand finally – FINALLY – moved up Kierra's thigh, between her legs and cupped her sex over her very skimpy underwear.

"How long have you been this wet?" Monica whispered.

"Three years," Kierra answered honestly.

Lane barked a laugh.

Monica moved her thumb over Kierra's clit and began to rub circles there. Kierra shivered and ground her hips down into Lane's very hard erection.

"Just this," Monica whispered. "The rest is for us."

Kierra didn't know what she meant until she moved away. This wasn't the mission. And no one in this skeevy Serbian club needed to see them finally get the exact thing they'd all been wanting for years.

Monica settled back down next to Lane, who kissed her and then whispered "Banovíc," just loud enough for them to hear.

They all turned and saw that Banovíc, flanked by his guards, had settled on the couch next to Stepanov. In the seconds – or minutes, Kierra was honestly unsure – when Kierra had been lost under the feel of Monica's hands and mouth on her, Stepanov had opened his pants and a man, who Kierra had not noticed before, was kneeling between his legs, sucking him off.

Stepanov and Banovíc raised their glasses to their small couch. Kierra had expected to feel panic rise in her chest at seeing him again. But she put on her mask and smiled, nodding her head slightly. Monica's hand between her legs and Lane's sure arm around her waist helped to calm her nerves.

seven

Kierra gave the Peters the four months' notice her contract required, but four months had felt so far away then. It was only just hitting her that in just a few days Monica and Lane wouldn't be her bosses anymore and it was hard to fathom. And even though quitting had been her idea, she still couldn't imagine her life without them. Especially not now, in the back of their hired car, as she leaned against Lane's chest, Monica's hand sliding between her legs and her eyes on her, deadly serious in a way that always made moisture pool at Kierra's center, as she lifted the poor excuse for a dress up her thighs.

"Is this what you want, sweet girl?" Lane asked, his voice still playful even if it did sound a bit ragged, like he was suppressing a growl. He ran his hand over Kierra's stomach in a soothing circle and then trailed his fingers lightly over her sternum.

"Yes," she moaned, trying to swivel her hips closer to Monica, but failing when Monica clutched her, holding her still.

"Are you sure?" Lane asked. Kierra turned to him and glared.

He laughed. "Tell her. Tell her exactly what you want."

Kierra turned back to Monica who was settled between her splayed legs. "I want you to taste me," she said. "Please."

If before tonight Monica had never smiled, she seemed to have an abundance of grins and smirks and smiles that almost bared her teeth, for Kierra. Monica licked her lips and then moved her fingers to the edge of Kierra's incredibly small thong. She ran her nail along that seam and Kierra groaned. When she pulled the fabric away, it clung to her wet sex. She blew on it softly and the brush of her breath made Kierra shiver, her hips straining toward Monica's face again.

The partition between them and the driver gave them the illusion of privacy. But since she'd just let Monica rub her to a gentle orgasm in the middle of an orgy while a high-ranking Serbian politician came in his boyfriend's mouth, what was a few moans in the car on the way home, Kierra thought.

And clearly Monica agreed. She lowered her head to Kierra's pussy, running her tongue through her folds and sucking her clit into her mouth. Kierra's hips jerked and she cried out, unable to stop herself. After three years of lust, it was finally happening. But then the car stopped. The driver's voice came through the intercom announcing that they had arrived back at the villa.

"Are you fucking kidding me?" Kierra yelled to no one in particular.

***

Kierra stumbled out of the car. Her high heels and wobbly legs made her feel like a drunk giraffe. Lane was at her back, an arm around her waist.

"Be careful there, sweet girl. Don't need you spraining an ankle," he said, with a soft chuckle.

Monica keyed in the code to the door and leaned down with wide eyes for the retinal scanner.

"Identity accepted," the digital voice intoned. Kierra had to bite her lip to keep from responding with her normal, "thanks, doll."

Inside the villa, Monica turned to Kierra and Lane, looking them over with lust in her eyes. Kierra's back was still pressed against Lane and she jumped when the front door closed behind them.

"You always wear those inappropriate shoes to work," Monica said, her gaze raking over Kierra's body.

"Well technically, tonight they were very appropriate," Lane replied in Kierra's defense. His free hand smoothed down her hip and then pulled up the hem of her dress slightly, his perfectly manicured fingernails scraping against her thigh. "But I sure do love to watch her prance around Command in them. The higher the better, if you ask me."

Kierra had spent three years in a near constant state of arousal. So when she realized that she had never been as turned on in her entire life, she knew that the bar was incredibly high. And yet, it was true. She was shaking in anticipation in Lane's arms and it only intensified as Monica stalked toward them.

She reached down and slid one hand along the seam of Kierra's thighs up toward the apex of her sex. Lane helpfully lifted Kierra's dress over her hips so that Monica could slip her hand into Kierra's panties. They really were a great team.

Kierra moaned as Monica's fingers lightly traced her folds, up and down, and then slipped gently into her opening. Kierra's head fell back onto Lane's shoulder.

"He loves when you're inappropriate," Monica whispered and then licked the column of Kierra's neck.

"I sure do," Lane concurred as he covered Kierra's mouth with his.

Kierra felt like one big exposed nerve ending. The heat of Lane's mouth, his tongue gliding along her own, Monica's finger - make that fingers – pumping into her were the stuff of her actual dreams. It didn't take long for her to come, her hips jerking on Monica's hand as Lane swallowed each and every one of her moans.

Kierra was shaking in Lane's arms, tiny spasms in her pussy still holding tight around Monica's fingers, when she finally broke away to gasp for air. Monica moved to kiss Lane. Kierra watched them, surprising herself by coming one more time, crushed between their bodies, Monica's fingers moving again as her palm ground into Kierra's clit, Lane's hard erection digging into the small of her back. She was so lost in the moment that the fear from earlier in the day felt like a nightmare from years ago.

***

Technically Lane and Monica were supposed to spend the next day out doing surveillance and checking in on their contacts and informants. To accomplish these mission objectives, they really needed to get to bed at a reasonable hour. And as their personal assistant, Kierra felt obligated to remind them of that. And she did. But her timing might have been off.

She and Monica were naked in bed.

"Tomorrow," she said just before Monica slipped her tongue into Kierra's mouth.

Kierra's hands were kneading Monica's breasts like she'd always dreamt of doing, rolling her nipples between her thumbs and forefingers. Monica broke the kiss and her head fell back as she groaned loudly. Kierra noticed that Lane was at Monica's back, a mischievous smile on his face. She looked down and was unsurprised to find his hand moving between Monica's legs.

"What about tomorrow, sweet girl?" He asked her the question as if this were a normal, regular day in the office. As if Monica wasn't shuddering through her orgasm between them. God, Kierra wished.

"You have contacts to meet. It's on your schedule."

Lane kept his eyes locked on Kierra's but moved his head to put a tender kiss on Monica's cheek. "Don't you worry about that, sweetness. We'll make our connects. Now get on your back."

Kierra shuddered. Lane never gave her commands. He asked nicely, in his most genteel Southern accent, preferring to let his tone cajole people into giving him what he wanted.

Monica demanded.

But maybe that was a sign of a great partnership, Kierra thought as she shifted back onto the bed, when one person is down – like Monica right now, in the beautifully incoherent afterglow of her orgasms – the other person picked up the slack. Kierra added this insight into their relationship as one more thing she loved about them. Monica's tongue flattened against her sex, lapping at her like she was the sweetest dessert. Kierra lost the train of her thoughts.

She could feel another orgasm coming on when Monica abruptly stopped. She grunted in frustration. When she opened her eyes, she had to close them again swiftly as the waves of her lust washed over her. She opened them again to check that was she saw was true. Lane kissing Monica, licking Kierra's essence off her tongue. They turned to her and Kierra could feel tiny spasms in her pussy, she'd always loved when they stared at her so intently. Monica kissed and licked her way up Kierra's body. When their mouths met, Monica whispered "sweet girl" against her lips, and kissed her. Kierra could have stayed like that all night, but her bosses had other plans.

Lane pulled a condom on and Monica straddled Kierra's head, facing Lane. Lane spread Kierra's legs, his hands behind her knees. She felt raw and exposed and beautiful. The feeling of Lane's cock sliding slowly into her and Monica settling her pussy over Kierra's mouth, her taste and scent engulfing her. It was everything that Kierra had been dreaming of for three years; Monica and Lane becoming her entire world.

eight

Maybe it was fate reminding her that all good things must come to an end, but Kierra felt as if the next thirty-six hours flew by.

Banovíc's party was tonight and after that Kierra would officially cease to be Monica and Lane's assistant. Her bosses still had to gather intel and meet with local contacts, but they refused to take Kierra with them; Lane had become downright paranoid about putting her in Banovíc's line of sight any more than was necessary. They hadn't told Kierra any specific mission details, but she knew that this trip had not been solely for reconnaissance, which meant that whatever their main objective was, Banovíc's private party was the most likely place for it to all come to a head.

The future was weighing heavy on Kierra's shoulders and, she liked to imagine, Monica and Lane's. At the very least, they all knew that the end of the mission and their professional relationship was fast approaching, and the villa became a hideaway from all that was to come. When Monica and Lane weren't out working, the three of them retreated to their bedroom, winding themselves around one other, touching and tasting and stroking until they were a sweaty, exhausted heap of tangled limbs. They showered and then started all over again.

But tonight was the night.

Kierra and Monica were lying on the bed, facing one another, kissing, lightly trailing their hands over one another's oiled bodies. They really didn't have much time. Kierra slipped her hand between Monica's leg's, circling her clit with the pads of her fingers, enjoying the way her normally stoic boss's icy exterior melted in ecstasy. Kierra wanted to kiss Monica, but she had so little time left with them that she leaned back to study her face, needing to commit this picture of Monica's release to memory alongside all the other images of her that Kierra could never forget.

The sound of a condom wrapper opening couldn't interrupt Kierra's concentration, but her heart did begin to beat faster. Lane lifted Kierra's leg and slid into her torturously slow. Their sex had ranged from hard and fast and filthy to a gentle, steady rock, but Kierra was certain that this was different. He ground his hips into her in deep strokes, as if he wanted Kierra to remember them later tonight, next week, next year. And she would.

She slipped two fingers into Monica, fucking her to the same rhythm as Lane fucked her. Lane buried his face in Kierra's neck, kissing and biting and sucking at her tender flesh, his panting loud in her ears, the vibration of his groans against her skin making her nipples painfully hard. They had to jump in the shower one more time to rinse off. They would be a bit late. But it was worth it.

***

When they arrived at Banovíc's private party at exactly midnight, Kierra was trying desperately to keep her emotions together. She felt absolutely beautiful in the see-through silk dress Lane had wanted her to wear that first night. The silk felt like clouds shifting over her body because she was completely bare underneath it. And even though Club Ménage was absolutely not her cup of tea, walking in on Monica and Lane's arms made Kierra feel sexy and powerful. She tried not to let it go to her head.

The party's atmosphere was hedonistic. The music was a slow, thumping techno beat that did nothing for her but apparently revved Eastern European engines, because everywhere she looked as they walked to their table, she saw every ménage configuration imaginable perched on the precipice of sexual explosion.

Kierra could also feel the subtle, menacing undercurrent of danger. It set her nerves on edge. She took deep calming breaths, willing herself to relax. It didn't hurt that Lane and Monica were armed to the hilt, which was surprising considering how, at a glance, there wouldn't seem to be any room for weaponry under their clothing. You know, if someone were looking for such a thing.

Monica was wearing a long-sleeved, floor length midnight blue velvet dress with a dangerously high slit up one thigh. So high that Kierra had been able to easily slide to the floor of their hired car and taste her, just one more time on the way to the party. Even with the long sleeves, that slit would certainly fool any corrupt member of the Serbian army into dismissing the possibilities for concealed weaponry. But when The Agency can make knives thin enough to not disturb the drape of a designer dress and technically, what was jewelry like Monica's spiky artistic necklace if not a collection of blades, said Serbian soldier would be a fool to dismiss Monica as less than a lethal and very efficient predator.

Lane's tuxedo, on the other hand, offered lots of opportunities for hiding a small arsenal and as far as Kierra could tell as she watched him slide guns and knives and spy gear into various hidden pockets and compartments, he'd taken advantage of every one of them.

They settled into a couch on the perimeter again, Kierra sitting in between Lane and Monica as before. This couch, Kierra realized only after they sat down, was better positioned than their previous position. It gave a perfect line of sight of the entrance, the door leading to the hallway where the bathrooms and an emergency exit were located as well as a door that Lane had whispered into her ear led to more private rooms upstairs. And, most importantly, there was a wall at their back, so they didn't have to worry about being surprised in that direction.

A waitress came over to them with a bottle of champagne. "Courtesy of President Banovíc," she said in a thick Russian accent, which Kierra noted sounded less harsh to her ears when compared to Serbian.

They all nodded and smiled in thanks, but none of them reached for it. Instead, they kept their eyes on the crowd of about two dozen people, surveying their surroundings and potential threats. Or at least that's what Lane and Monica were probably doing. Kierra was in it for the action. Sometimes Lane leaned over to kiss Kierra's neck so that he could relay some observation to them while hiding his mouth. And every now and then, Monica would turn and kiss one or the other of them, to do the same.

And then Banovíc walked into the room to everyone's applause. Kierra clapped half-heartedly, her body suddenly tense and her mind alert. "Here we go," she whispered to herself.

Lane kissed her ear and grabbed her wrist to put an elegant, sleek bracelet on her arm. When Kierra peered at it closely, she realized that it was a digital timer. He whispered loud enough for Monica to hear, "I've set an alarm to go off at exactly 2:00. I don't care where we are or what we're doing, when that alarm goes off you head straight for the emergency exit."

Kierra turned to him with wide eyes.

"With or without us, sweet girl," Monica whispered into her ear.

Kierra swung to her, angry and sad, but not entirely sure why. What else had she expected? They were spies and this was a mission. She wanted to shake her head and yell at them that they were heartless. That they should have told her the plan sooner. That she deserved to know the operation details. But even if she deserved to know, she definitely didn't have the security clearance to get it. And they didn't have time for an outburst.

Banovíc's guards set a chair shaped not unlike a throne across from them and he lowered his body, clad in yet another ill-fitting uniform, into it.

Kierra tamped down on her own anger, burying it as deep as it could go, and turned a smiling, but aloof, face to Banovíc.

"President Banovíc," Lane said in a much deeper Southern accent than Kierra had ever heard, "This is an honor."

Unsurprisingly, those words stroked the dictator's fragile, xenophobic ego and he preened accordingly.

"Mr. and Mrs. Hudson and," he turned toward Kierra, "Laura, I am so happy you could make it."

His smile was predatory. He clearly wanted to show them all that he had done his homework and knew everything about them. By the way he bared his teeth at Kierra, she guessed that he wanted her to be particularly unnerved. But since it took her a few seconds to remember that Laura was the name on her fake passport for this trip, she only smiled wider at him and then turned to lick and kiss Monica's neck, snuggling close. She ignored Banovíc's animalistic grunt.

"I would like to invite you upstairs to my private room," Banovíc said, his lust dripping from every word.

Kierra was happy that she had buried her face in Monica's hair because her eyes bulged at the invitation. This sounded like an absolutely terrible idea. She held her breath, waiting for Monica or Lane to answer.

Monica reached up and cupped the back of Kierra's head, stroking her strands gently, clearly having noticed the tension in her body. "We would be delighted," she said in the softest voice Kierra had ever heard pass her lips, if she didn't count the soft mewling sighs she made after she came.

"Wonderful," Banovíc said, clapping his hands. "Please. Follow me."

Kierra gripped Monica's hand tightly as her boss followed Banovíc down a sterile hallway at the top of a narrow flight of stairs. Lane was at her back, a reassuring hand on her waist. Behind him, only one of Banovíc's guards, the one who had approached them that first night, followed.

pink slip

Kierra didn't know anything about being a spy, but she would have assumed that if there was a handbook, it would certainly say that following a despot into a private room with an armed guard was Bad Idea 101. They had absolutely no idea who was up here. What if their cover actually had been blown? What if Banovíc was leading them away to have them killed or captured and tortured? All these thoughts were running through her head and she decided that, freaky sex aside, she much preferred being an impoverished poet to the spy life. And right now it seemed a better vocation than even being two powerful spies' personal assistant. Less guns and knives; more books and tea.

They reached the end of the hall and Banovíc opened a very ordinary door that Kierra imagined was a portal into hell. When they'd stepped into the room, Banovíc's personal guard didn't cross the threshold. He simply nodded at his boss and pulled the door shut. Kierra assumed he would be acting sentry.

She looked around the room and frowned. It was dominated by a large four poster bed, ugly antique rugs and a sitting area with another gaudy plush couch in front of a fireplace. She rolled her eyes at the club's continued terrible taste.

"That's it?" She asked, in an annoyed voice. "It's just us?"

There was a moment of silence where Kierra realized that she'd said that out loud. Monica's face was still pleasant and smiling, but Kierra saw the slight tension around the corner of her eyes. And Lane's face was amused, but he was always amused, although Kierra noticed that he'd moved his hands to his hips and closer to the gun at his back.

She turned to Banovíc whose gnarled face seemed puzzled. She smiled and then said, "I thought there would be other people here for us to play with." And just like that, the moment of tension seemed to dissipate.

Banovíc clapped and turned to Lane, "She's a greedy girl, I take it?"

Lane nodded at Kierra, his eyes full of affectionate indulgence, "You have no idea."

Banovíc's attention zeroed in on Kierra and his eyes roamed over her body appreciatively. She tried not to heave. "Don't worry, little bird, I am more than enough for you."

He tore his eyes away from Kierra and turned back to Lane. "Mr. Hudson," Banovíc said in a dark tone, "I would very much like to play with your little pet. She has informed me that I need your permission."

Lane's easygoing smile didn't falter. "It would be an honor," he said. Banovíc didn't waste a second of hesitation before heading toward her. Lane's voice stopped him short. "However, I'm afraid the person you have to ask for permission to touch our girl is my wife."

"Oh?" Kierra already hated Banovíc, but his startled grunt only heightened her dislike. He was annoyed.

He turned to Monica then, openly ogling her. He walked toward her, reaching for her hand. She offered it willingly, and then he bent down to kiss and lick her knuckles.

Kierra had to swallow a gag at the sight. Monica's alluring smile never wavered. "My dear Mrs. Hudson, may I play with your beautiful little bird?"

Monica placed her hands on either side of Banovíc's face. "I would be offended if you did not," she said. And then kissed him. Kierra's eyes went wide at the sight and the panic in her breast began to build.

What if he touched her? What if they let him?

Monica pulled away from the kiss and Banovíc's face was overjoyed. Kierra struggled to keep the smile on her face as he turned toward her. Monica kept her hands on his shoulders as he advanced on Kierra, encouraging him along.

When he reached her, Kierra's heart was pumping hard and fast in her chest. She was terrified. "Beautiful," he whispered. She closed her eyes and shivered. He seemed to think that was a good thing. She began to count down, waiting for the moment when his rough, probably sweaty hands stained with the blood of helpless refugees touched her. She knew she would scream.

But it never came.

Kierra peeked one eye open and then the other. There was a needle sticking out of Banovíc's neck and his eyes were wild with fear and confusion.

Lane moved quickly, helping Monica get him across the room and onto the bed. Kierra tried to process everything as it happened, but she wasn't sure exactly *what* was happening, so that was difficult.

Once on the bed, Lane began unbuckling Banovíc's pants and pulled them down over his hips, exposing his small flaccid penis. Monica took a pouch from a strap wrapped around her thigh. Inside was a collection of syringes and a vial.

"What's that?" Kierra hissed and then glanced at the door, hoping that the guard hadn't heard.

When she turned back, Monica was filling the syringe with whatever was in the vial. She tied a small rope around Banovíc's bicep, just above the crook of his elbow and began trying to coax a vein to the surface of his skin. She pushed the needle into his arm and depressed the syringe slowly, carefully. Lane had undone the buttons of his shirt. He pressed two fingers to Banovíc's other wrist. They all stayed like that, silently waiting, until finally Lane announced that he was dead.

So that was the mission, Kierra belatedly realized.

Lane looked at Monica and nodded. Monica climbed from the bed and pulled the top of her dress down over her shoulders, exposing her breasts. She grabbed Kierra by the shoulders, "Almost over, sweet girl. Just a little bit more."

She moved to the door and wrenched it open. "Something's wrong with him," she said to the guard, who automatically rushed inside. "His heart," she said and touched her breast to mime the word. The guard's attention was so focused on her naked flesh that he dropped without ever seeing Lane pull the gun from his waist. Kierra hadn't even heard the shot. When she turned to Lane, she was momentarily surprised to see the gun in his hand and the large silencer on the tip.

He wiped his fingerprints off the gun and placed it on the bed next to Banovíc. "Let's go," he announced.

If anyone should ever have cause to ask her, Kierra was fully prepared to lie and say that the shock of watching her bosses kill two men – like the trained spy-assassins they were – deeply traumatized her. She would say that Lane had to basically carry her out of that room because she was rooted in place, paralyzed by shock and unable to fully comprehend what had happened.

In reality, she had picked up the hem of her long dress and high-tailed it out of that room behind Monica without a second thought, skipping over the dead guard who she was sure was just following orders. Or whatever. Lane closed the door behind them and then knelt down, pulled a lock picking set from his jacket pocket and locked it. They hustled down the hallway to the stairs.

The staircase was enclosed between two doors. Monica opened it slowly, peering around the corner. No one was there. They descended quietly, but quickly. Just as Monica was reaching for the door that would lead them back into Club Ménage's main room, the digital timer on Kierra's wrist went off. Kierra raised her arm and stared at it as if the timer and her arm were made of alien alloy. Lane reached around, shut the timer off and slipped it off her wrist.

He turned her around and cupped her face. "Well, I guess this is the end of the road, sweet girl." He still had that same easy smile on his face and for the first time Kierra hated it.

Tears sprang to her eyes.

"The driver is going to pick you up at the back of the club. Go out of the emergency exit, down the alley and he'll be there with a change of clothes," Monica said.

"No," Kierra said without thinking.

"He'll take you straight to the airport. Our jet will take you home," Lane finished.

"No," Kierra said louder, but still not loud enough to draw attention, just in case.

"This was your idea, Kierra," Monica said.

"But that was before." She didn't finish the sentence. It was obvious. That was before the last two days, before this trip. She'd never told them why she wanted to leave and she didn't have to. It was clear. As their personal assistant, Lane and Monica would never cross lines the way they had done this entire week. Being with them was too dangerous. No matter how much they wanted each other. No matter how high her heels or how tight her skirts or how many times they called her 'sweet girl' like an erotic endearment. Whoever they worked for would not approve. Their line of work was far too dangerous for an aspiring poet with low-level security clearance.

Kierra knew that. But she wanted them to say that it didn't matter.

Lane leaned down to kiss her instead. It was a hard press of his mouth, his tongue sliding roughly against hers, his semi-hard dick pressed against her mound.

And then it was Monica's turn. Her mouth was gentler, but no less greedy. Her hands roamed over Kierra's body, sliding that thin silk around her overheated flesh.

It was over all too soon. "We're gonna miss you," Monica whispered in her hard and demanding voice, as if she understood just how much Kierra needed to hear it just one more time.

And then Monica turned and opened the door.

"Take care of yourself, sweet girl," Lane whispered into her ear and then moved past her into the club, his hand going around Monica's waist. They didn't look back.

Kierra slipped down the hallway, smiling politely at the women and men who admired her nearly naked body openly, fighting tears the whole way. She turned around to make sure that the hallway was clear before she pushed the door open into the night.

She lifted her dress to keep it from the muck of the alley. Out on the main drag, their hired car was there. The chauffeur opened the door, coolly and professionally. He didn't rush her into the back seat. He didn't run back to the driver's side. He drove at a reasonable speed until he turned the corner away from the club and then he sped away. Kierra wasn't sure what the speed limit was in Novi Sad, but if there was one, their driver exceeded it by a lot. And she was thankful that he did.

Kierra found the bag with her clothing on the seat next to her. She raised the partition and pulled out the same outfit she'd just five days ago been agonizing over in front of her floor-length mirror. She slid into her underwear, pulled on her bra, slipped the cropped band t-shirt over her head. She shimmied into the pencil skirt but was happy to find a pair of flats inside. She didn't have the heart for a pair of skinny heels right now. She also found her purse, which held her real passport, wallet and cell phone. There was also that purple dress that Monica loved and the mesh dress that, even after everything that had happened, made her sex clench as she remembered Monica's fingers between her legs and Lane's hard cock beneath her. She felt tears pushing at the back of her eyes as she pushed the beautiful silk dress into the bag and zipped it closed. The pressure of tears was almost painful, but she refused to give into them. Not yet.

At the airport, she sped through the security line. Apparently, Serbia didn't care so much about foreigners leaving. She boarded Monica and Lane's jet and they were in the air in no time. Kierra walked to the back of the plane to the bedroom and collapsed onto the bed. It seemed impossible to believe, but she was no longer Monica and Lane Peters' personal assistant. She finally let the tears fall down her face and then fell asleep alone.

pink slip

PART TWO

nine

Kierra was depression cleaning.

She was unemployed, hadn't written a word in over a week and sitting around idly was playing havoc with her brain. But that wasn't what was fueling her mood. She missed Monica and Lane. It had been over a week since she'd slipped out of Club Ménage and she'd foolishly thought that they would contact her. But apparently that wasn't how spies operated. Go figure.

When she arrived home, she found all the small knickknacks she'd brought to work had been returned. There was a picture of her parents, a picture of her and Maya at their college graduation, a cactus that she'd somehow managed to keep alive for two years and a Batgirl bobblehead Monica and Lane had given her for her one-year anniversary as their PA. Everything was in a box on her kitchen table, with an impersonal letter thanking her for three years of service on stationary with a letterhead from a company she'd never heard of. The finality of that letter and the box of her things sent her to bed for four days. She'd only managed to pull herself upright when her roommate Maya accidentally set off the fire alarm while making a grilled cheese sandwich. Mentally she was still lying in that bed, leaking tears.

But now that she was up, she decided to make the best of this brief reprieve from her crippling sadness by giving the kitchen a good scrub and disinfecting literally every surface. The smell of bleach stung her eyes, which her mother had always considered a sign that you were on the right path. An emo playlist of rhythm & blues ballads about heartbreak, inventively titled "Tracks of My Tears" was blaring through the Bluetooth speaker.

Kierra was on her hands and knees scrubbing the space between the fridge and the counter when the music abruptly shut off. She turned to find Maya standing over her, clearly pissed.

Maya was half-dressed in a skimpy lace bodysuit that showed off her thick thighs and slightly rounded stomach and made her breasts look absolutely amazing. She had a full face of soft makeup that most men would assume wasn't makeup at all and her dyed honey blonde hair was styled in tousled waves.

Kierra nodded her approval. "Cute," she said.

Maya dropped the hand on her hip and smiled, "I know, right?" Maya could never resist a compliment. But then she got back to business. "So look Kiki, I realize that you're going through something and you don't want to tell me. And that's chill, no pressure, I'm here whenever you're ready.

But girl, this loud ass music reminds me of when my mama used to break up with her trifling boyfriends and sit in her room drinking brown liquor, chain smoking Newports. And girl," she said, letting that word trail on for a few seconds, "that is not the kind of mood I need to hear when I'm working."

Kierra sighed. "Sorry, I'll keep it down."

Maya scrunched her face, "God, don't sound so sad when you say it. Now I feel bad."

Kierra stood, pulled the large yellow rubber gloves from her hands and threw them into the sink. "Don't feel bad. I'm just... I just need some time," she finished quietly.

"This is about your bosses, right?"

Kierra nodded.

"Do you want to tell me what happened on your trip?"

Kierra shook her head.

Maya opened her mouth to speak and then the alarm in her room started going off. "Shit, I have to go," she said, gesturing toward her bedroom. "I have a broadcast starting in a few. I don't want to keep my viewers waiting."

"The glamorous life of a cam model," Kierra said, a small smile on her face.

"Don't knock it. It pays my half of the bills and keeps Sallie Mae off my back."

Kierra put up her hands in surrender. "No judgement. If you like it, I love it."

Maya looked at her for a second, the alarm still blaring from her bedroom. "Actually," she said, "you really might be into it."

Kierra laughed and shook her head. It was her first real laugh in what felt like years. "Oh no, that's your thing. Don't try and pull me in."

Maya shrugged and walked out of the kitchen. Just before she disappeared down their short hallway, she turned to Kierra and said in the voice that must drive some of her clients wild, "If you ever change your mind, you know where to find me."

She winked. Kierra burst out laughing. Her best friend was the absolute best.

***

Kierra started to feel normal again after a month. Well, as normal as she could feel while unemployed and trying to process a kinda sorta breakup. She started leaving the house on a regular basis although she mostly just sat in coffee shops, trying to write, but just scribbling Monica and Lane's names over and over again – sometimes putting her own in between them – instead. It was very high school dramatics, but Kierra had decided to lean into it.

She had just wasted a few hours at a new coffee shop in her neighborhood and was walking slowly home, feeling highly caffeinated and very sorry for herself. It was a nice fall day in Jersey, crisp, cool air, orangey-red leaves falling from trees; very Lifetime movie set. Kierra was daydreaming about the leaves being the almost exact same bright red color as the lipstick Monica had been wearing the last time they had all been together in bed. She could feel her body heat as she remembered what the color had looked like smeared over Lane's mouth.

She began to unwind the light scarf tangled around her neck. A loud car crash at the intersection behind her made her jump and her heart race. She turned around to see the collision. In the center of the intersection, two almost indistinguishable gray sedans were crumpled together in a sickening heap of rent metal. Kierra watched as a man from one of the cars jumped onto the street and moved to the other car. He leaned into the window briefly and then turned to scream at the slowly growing crowd of useless onlookers, "Someone call an ambulance!"

Kierra pulled her phone from the back pocket of her jeans and started to call when someone bumped into her left side from behind. The girl who brushed past her was wearing a simple pair of jeans and a thin gray t-shirt. She turned around, a smile on her face, and murmured an apology. It was such an ordinary moment, but the hair on Kierra's arms were standing straight up as if there was electricity in the air.

Kierra put her phone back into her pocket, turned and walked home as quickly as she could without running so as not to draw any unnecessary attention to herself. All while stealing glances over her shoulder to make sure that she wasn't being followed. When she was finally back at her apartment, she slipped her key into the lock, looked both ways down her hallway, and then turned the handle to let herself inside, swiftly closing the door behind her. She quickly locked all three door locks, plus the chain, and turned to lean her back against the door. Her heart was racing. The sound of Maya's laughter made her jump.

"Oh my god, you're a freaky one," Maya whispered to herself, her cell phone clutched in her hands as she walked into the living room. She looked up and absently waved at Kierra. "When'd you get back?"

Kierra swallowed and tried to force a lightness in her voice that she didn't feel. "Just now."

"Cool," she replied, still engrossed in her phone.

"Who are you talking to?" Kierra asked, pushing away from the door and following Maya into their small kitchen, needing to be close to someone she trusted after the eerie feeling that had chased her home.

"New client negotiations. He seems fun," Maya replied, looking up at Kierra with a dirty smile on her face.

Kierra rolled her eyes.

"Oh, you got a letter earlier," Maya said. "It's on the coffee table."

Kierra walked into the living room on suddenly shaky legs. When she reached the coffee table, she let out a sigh of relief. She picked up the large envelope, tore it open and pulled out her welcome packet from the Enniskerry Writers Retreat.

"What is it?" Maya asked, walked back toward her bedroom, a cup of water in one hand, her phone in the other, typing quickly with her thumb; a small smile on her face.

"It's from the writing retreat I'm going to."

"Ooh, I forgot you were leaving me again."

"Not for another couple of months," Kierra said, sifting through the packet of information, letting the excitement pull her fully out of the mire of her own irrational paranoia and persistent sadness.

"I hope it lifts your mood," Maya replied. Kierra turned toward her and gave her best friend her most convincing smile. "And I also hope you get laid."

Kierra laughed and grabbed a cushion from the couch to throw at her friend, who dodged it easily. "Hey, I have a few clients who'd be interested in a pillow fight. Let me know if you're down."

"Go away," Kierra yelled around her own laughter.

"Don't say I never tried to put you on," Maya yelled and then closed her bedroom door; her laughter carrying through the thin walls.

Kierra turned back to her mail and smiled softly to herself. And then, because her brain just refused to give her a moment of peace, she wondered where Monica and Lane were, because she missed them terribly.

ten

"Is twenty-seven too young to be having a mid-life crisis?" Kierra posed the question to her phone's voice recorder because the last time she'd asked her best friend that question, Maya had rolled her eyes so hard she'd almost dislodged a fake eyelash. So she found no help there. But the question still lingered. How could it not?

She was currently standing in the passenger pick-up section in Terminal 2 at Dublin Airport waiting for the shuttle that would take her to the very expensive writing retreat in the Irish countryside. All through graduate school, this retreat had been her singular obsession because her graduate mentor, Gwendolyn Miles, had insisted that this retreat had allowed her to draft most of a new collection of poems and short stories that then went on to win the prestigious Brooks-Giovanni Poetry Prize. Being able to afford this retreat had always seemed like a goalpost that Kierra thought would indicate her commitment to her art and put her on the path her mentor had laid out for her. She'd psyched herself into believing that she would not be a true poet until she bled – figuratively, financially – for her craft.

And after five years of dreaming, she was about to live out one of her dreams just as soon as the retreat shuttle arrived. But just three months after saying goodbye to her former bosses in a Serbian sex club immediately after they'd killed the president and his personal bodyguard… life felt a little strange. On the one hand, as the now former personal assistant to a pair of international spies, with actual money in her checking *and* savings accounts, her days were much less demanding. She slept in when she wanted. She didn't have to have her apartment swept for listening and recording devices on a regular basis. She'd mostly stopped fearing that she was being tailed. And without her former bosses' all-consuming presence in her life Monday through Friday, most weekends with the occasional international trip, she had stopped wearing the tightest clothes and highest heels in her closet. Because there was no one left to impress.

And Kierra was bored.

"So yeah... really, is twenty-seven too young for a mid-life crisis?" She asked her voice memo app again. It wouldn't provide any answers and so was about as helpful as Maya, but maybe if she said it in different intonations, stressing various words, she'd stumble upon an answer. Or a poem.

Kierra let out an exasperated sigh and checked the watch on her left wrist. When she looked up, a very ugly shuttle bus was pulling into the passenger pick-up area. It was painted a pastel blue and covered in dozens of children's drawings on the side. Kierra raised an eyebrow and, when the bus stopped in front of her, she reared back in shock. The door opened and the driver descended the stairs with a wide smile on his face. Aimed directly at her.

"The hell you say," Kierra said before she could stop herself.

"Are you Kierra?" He asked in a slightly high-pitched American accent that she knew would give her a headache inside of five minutes.

She scanned him from head to toe. He was Asian with a strong jaw and a smile that would have been pleasant if it were slightly less wide. He was tall and looked muscular, she thought, although it was hard to tell what was beneath the ugliest outfit she'd ever seen in her life. He wore a fishing hat (for no apparent reason), a utility vest (also for no apparent reason) over a t-shirt that was a shade of green that made his skin look gray and dull, and cargo pants (honestly, how many pockets does one person need!?). But the worst part, as far as Kierra was concerned, were his ugly sandals, that looked to be made of hemp, on his socked feet.

She began to shake her head immediately.

pink slip

His smile faltered for a second, but then it was back to its former uncomfortable width. "Kierra Ward? Am I saying that right?"

Kierra took a deep breath and then nodded, resigning herself to the sure reality that this retreat was maybe not going to be all that she'd hoped.

"Yes, sorry," she said, forcing a smile. "I'm Kierra Ward. Are you from the Enniskerry Writers Retreat?"

"I am," he replied with a very satisfied look on his face. "I'm the new social director, Kenny Wu." He stuck his hand out and she tentatively reached out to shake it. He grasped her small hand and shook so hard he nearly took her off her feet.

"Ow. Okay, we can stop now, Hulk," she yelled.

He immediately released her and his cheeks reddened. "Sorry. Sometimes I don't know my own strength. Well, we should get going. It's a thirty-minute drive to the countryside." And with that he hefted her very heavy suitcase as if it weighed nothing and walked back onto the bus.

Kierra took another deep breath and looked around her in a move that had become a sad habit since Serbia. It was an unfortunate by-product not of being Monica and Lane's assistant, but of having very briefly been their lover. She knew what they were capable of. If they wanted, they could have located her anywhere in the world. If they wanted, they could have tracked her down and asked her to come back. But they hadn't. And Kierra was sad and angry about that more and more every day.

Just as she started to frown, a flash of movement in her peripheral vision caught her eye. She scanned a small crowd gathered at a taxi stand, all waiting impatiently. A family with two screaming children were at its head. The mother seemed to be trying to placate them, while the father checked his watch and looked anxiously away as if he were late for something, while two teenage girls posed for a selfie.

"Ready?" Kenny called from the bus.

Kierra gave him a weak smile and stepped off the curb.

eleven

"Am I having a psychotic break?" Kierra typed into the search engine on her phone. She was currently hiding in a window seat, crouched behind a heavy and musty old curtain in the library of the old – and very drafty, she was going to make sure to mention on the retreat's comment card – house in the small Irish town of Enniskerry. The highlights of this town seemed to be pigs, wild chickens, a rooster that couldn't discern between daybreak and two o'clock in the afternoon, and dial-up internet.

She'd been at the writing retreat for two days and had become certain of a few things. First, she was right, four minutes into the thirty-minute drive from the airport, Kenny's voice had coaxed a splitting migraine to blossom just behind her right temple. She'd hoped that it might disappear once they arrived at the villa, but as social director, he was literally everywhere and was literally always talking. Second, between her migraine, very little sleep – on account of the wind gusting through every crack in her room – and the hunger, she hadn't written one word at this very expensive retreat and she wouldn't if things didn't change. And thirdly, about the hunger: Irish food was terrible. Or at least their Irish chef was terrible. But Kierra couldn't be bothered to split hairs when she could literally feel her stomach eating itself.

The little dotted circle at the top of her phone screen turned and turned for a solid five minutes before the webpage finally loaded a results page with several interesting lists and online quizzes to her query. She couldn't click on anything, lest that page take another five minutes to load, but from what she gleaned on just the results page, all the websites seemed to be suggesting that... maybe she was having a nervous breakdown. But also, maybe she wasn't. She chewed her lip and tried to quell the rising panic that she'd wasted a sizeable chunk of her unemployment nest egg to not eat or sleep in a farm town in rural Ireland and not write one word.

She started typing a very angry, but carefully worded, email to her mentor asking if *this* was really the retreat that had changed her life, when she heard it. She clutched her phone to her chest and held her breath.

It was Kenny. She knew it was. It was always Kenny.

He seemed to follow her around the grounds as if she were the only guest at the retreat. Every time she turned around, there he was, "checking in". How was she supposed to write if he hovered? Another thing she would be complaining about at the end of the retreat in just five more days. Five drafty days without a meal worth swallowing.

The steps were slow and measured as whoever it was behind the curtain walked into the room. Kierra held her breath and prayed they would move on. But they didn't. The footsteps grew closer. Kierra's heart was beating fast in her chest and she could feel beads of sweat at her hairline. She closed her eyes, childishly hoping the person would disappear or that she would remain invisible.

And then there were other footsteps in the room.

"Kenny," Asif Hassan said, his Irish accent thick and, when he really got going, almost musical.

Kierra let out the breath she'd been holding slowly, silently; relief washing over her.

"The pigs have gotten out of the pen, mate."

Kierra could hear the sneer in Kenny's voice, which was not as high-pitched as normal and so didn't aggravate her migraine as much. "That's not my job."

There was a moment of silence between them, longer than Kierra thought there should be. Finally, Kenny let out an exaggerated sigh. "Fine. But this is not what I'm paid to do."

Kierra listened as his footsteps faded into the distance, but she refused to move. And then the heavy curtain was ripped away.

pink slip

"There you are," Asif said, his tan face smiling down at her. His jet-black hair was in an artfully disheveled bun on the top of his head and he looked as he normally did, devastatingly handsome and a little bit mischievous.

She smiled up at him, "How did you know I was back here?"

"Easy. I just thought 'where would I hide if Kenny was trying to convince me to do a journaling exercise about marmalade'? And here you are." He reached out his hand to her and she happily grasped it to steady herself as she stood up.

"He just won't leave me alone," Kierra whined. "Everywhere I go, he's right there. This is not the retreat I was expecting. Were you?"

She asked the question and looked pleadingly into his eyes. She didn't like to plead, but she was very close to her wits' end. Also, she simply enjoyed looking at him. Especially when he smiled at her as if she were the only person in the room. Although, she realized, and took a step back pulling her hand from his, she actually was the only other person in the room so there was no need to let herself get carried away. Besides, there was the other matter of her still being pathetically hung up on her former bosses.

If Asif noticed that awkward moment, he didn't comment on it. Instead he smiled and answered her question. "I don't have expectations. They're too difficult to manage. I take everything as it comes."

"And how's that working out with this retreat?"

"Well," he said, leading her out of the library in the opposite direction of the pig pens behind the building. "Kenny is a right knob and hours of entertainment. And you're literally gorgeous. So I think this retreat is turning out just fine."

He beamed at Kierra as they walked slowly downstairs, through the sitting room just off the main entrance and into the breakfast room that everyone used as a lounge since that's where the coffee was.

She rolled her eyes and shook her head. "Ugh, optimism."

Asif's laugh was a nice, deep rumble that didn't ask anything of her, not even unbidden arousal. It just washed over her, comforting her distress and inviting her not to take the retreat – or life – so seriously. Not for the first time in the last couple of days, Kierra tried to ignore the way Asif reminded her of Lane.

***

Kierra was having a good dream. A great dream actually. Besides the bliss of passing out and staying asleep even as it sounded like a tornado was ravaging the old house's rafters, this was an A+ dream. It was a snatch of a memory mixed with a bit of fantasy.

She shivered in her sleep, remembering the way Lane's eyes had roamed appreciatively over her body, his hands sliding up Monica's back between them. She knew the moment that he entered Monica because she moaned, guttural and deep, and the vibrations had washed over Kierra's sex and sent her spiraling over the edge. But that memory transformed into a fantasy.

They were having breakfast at Command. Monica and Lane were sitting across from one another in the boardroom, strategizing and comparing intel, their eyes drinking in Kierra's body, barely covered in that mesh dress. She pranced around the table in her highest, thinnest heels and poured coffee, offered Monica another pen just as the one she was using began to run out and straightened stacks of files Lane had spread haphazardly on the table.

Kierra sometimes felt ridiculous that this was the kind of thing that got her off: anticipating Monica and Lane's needs while desperately displaying herself in front of them; for them. But she had been their PA for three years and had spent the entire time drowning in her own lustful fantasies. Just as it had taken a while after she left school to stop waking up in the middle of the night in a cold sweat worried that she still needed to finish a phantom essay or prepare for a test tomorrow, she needed some time to adjust to this transition. In the meantime, her dreams were a psychoanalyst's financial windfall.

She was just getting to the good part. Sitting demurely in Monica's lap, Kierra was all but purring. Monica lightly stroked her thighs as she and Lane discussed the best tactic for breaking into the Chinese embassy in South Africa; as if this were oh so normal. Because that was Kierra's ultimate fantasy. She gasped in her dream, and in reality, when Monica's fingers grazed the edge of her pussy.

"Keep quiet, sweet girl," Lane said, his voice a promise of what would come if she didn't.

And Kierra tried, biting her lips and swallowing the moans that threatened to break free as Monica gently massaged the skin where her leg met her hip, starting at the outer edge and pushing down between her legs, just barely grazing her sex. But then Monica pushed her legs apart so that she had a better angle to rub her clit in hard circles just as she announced that she needed Kierra to order her a new sniper scope. And Kierra had to answer her, it was her job. Only when she opened her mouth a loud moan escaped instead of the "On it," she had meant to say. Lane was standing up, looking at her with hard eyes and that easy smile, slowly unbuckling his belt. And Monica's fingers had slipped inside of her.

A loud crash from the garden pulled Kierra from her dream and she sat straight up in bed, panting, a light sheen of sweat on her upper lip.

She looked around her dark room. Everything looked as it should be in the dim light from the moon through the windows. There were no new sounds outside and she almost wondered if she hadn't dreamt the crash that startled her awake. But her racing heart and raised hairs on her arms told her that she had heard something. The wind howled outside and seeped through the poorly framed windows. She decided to assume that the relentless gusting air was the culprit as she settled back into bed. She tossed and turned, trying desperately to get back what she had lost.

twelve

Kierra was bleary eyed.

She spent half the night angrily awake and horny only to drift into a deep sleep just as the sun had begun to rise. She also missed breakfast. From the previous three days, she felt certain that the eggs would have been runny or insanely dry and the toast and sausage would very likely have been burnt beyond recognition. But her stomach growled loudly that even that might have been worth it. She was also late for the early freewriting exercises; the only time Kenny left her alone long enough to think.

She could see everyone filing down the hall toward the large conference room they used for group writing and turned in the other direction toward the kitchen. She couldn't stop the triumphant yelp from escaping her lips when she saw a carafe of coffee. She pressed her hand to its side, and it was hot and likely fresh. It wasn't her mama's grits and eggs, but it would do. For a brief moment Kierra thought that maybe this was going to be the turning point of this retreat. Maybe she'd write a few lines. Maybe the cook would finally make something better than mostly edible. Maybe her heartbreak would miraculously heal.

But then a few things happened all at once to send her day into a tailspin.

First, outside in the garden the chickens started to squawk loudly. Kierra moved to the sink to peer out of the window, which is why she didn't notice the man inching toward her through the kitchen's back door with a knife in his hand. So in hindsight she guessed he counted as the second thing. But she didn't notice any of the danger at her back until the third thing happened: the cook, the absolutely terrible cook named Mrs. Wilde – who seemed hell bent on keeping her hungry and agitated – burst out of the pantry and clubbed the man over the head with a heavy rolling pin. His knife clattered to the kitchen floor.

Kierra jumped and turned, her eyes wide and her heart racing. She took in the scene in front of her and absolutely none of it made sense. "What the fuck?"

The rolling pin in Mrs. Wilde's hand was bloody. She kicked the knife out of the man's reach and leaned down to check his pulse.

"Mrs. Wilde, what the fuck is going on?" Kierra screamed. The cook ignored her.

Asif came running into the kitchen, Kenny fast on his heels.

"Help me get him up," Mrs. Wilde directed, and Asif moved to the prone body on the floor.

"Are you all right?" Kenny was standing in front of Kierra, squatting down to her eye level and peering into her face, his hands gripping her shoulders.

She was shaking. "What the fuck?" was all she could think to say again.

"I said, are you all right?" Kenny asked louder.

"She's in shock, not deaf, you idiot," Asif said as he and Mrs. Wilde pushed the unconscious man into a chair. He slumped face first onto the table.

Kierra turned quickly toward them, her eyes bulging. "Where the fuck is your accent?" She asked Asif, who until right this moment had spent the past two days trying to charm her with an Irish accent that was missing in action this morning. Apparently. They all stopped. Mrs. Wilde looked between Asif and Kenny and Kierra, her mouth a thin, serious line.

Asif stood up; hands held out in front of him. "Okay, there's something we need to tell you," he started in a very thick Boston accent.

Kierra bolted out of the kitchen before any of them could react. She heard two pairs of footsteps behind her, but she could see the front door in front of her. She reached out for the knob, willing it closer. And then she was being lifted off of her feet. She started screaming.

"Calm down, Kierra," Asif said in his new accent.

"Put me down," she screamed back.

"Sorry folks, nothing to see here. Just an exercise on finding your voice. Get ready," Kenny said in his normal, high-pitched, social director voice. Kierra assumed he was talking to the other retreat participants. She screamed.

Asif had one arm around her waist, and she tried desperately to shake her head to stop him from covering her mouth. But Kenny grasped her ankles. She gasped and Asif finally muffled her screams. They shuffled her upstairs to her drafty bedroom before she even had time to fully comprehend all that had happened.

Asif kicked the door closed behind them. Kenny clutched her ankles with one surprisingly strong hand and used the other to strip the thin blanket from her bed. He used it to tie her legs together so that Asif could hold her on his own. Kenny pulled up her sheets and began ripping them into long strips they used to tie her to the hard, straight-backed chair in the corner of her room.

Only when her arms and legs were restrained did Kierra realize that maybe she didn't just get to walk away from being the personal assistant to spies. Maybe it wasn't that easy. She was scared and then angry as hell. Shouldn't Monica and Lane have told her that when they accepted her resignation? If she ever got out of this situation, she was going to write them a very strongly worded email and send it to their encrypted email server. Their new assistant would probably delete it on sight, assuming they hadn't changed all their servers the day after she left. But still, she'd write it because this was really fucked up.

Kenny crouched down in front of her, his ears red, she hoped in shame. "I'm really sorry. This wasn't supposed to happen this way."

Kierra wanted to scream at him and ask exactly how this was supposed to go down. But there was a gag in her mouth, so she glared at him instead.

Asif pulled his cell phone from his pocket, pressed a button and waited for someone to answer. "Echo 5, Protocol B," was all he said before hanging up again. Kierra didn't recognize that operative combination.

He turned to Kierra and gave her an awkward smile. "So you really bought my accent?"

Kenny groaned as he stood. "You've gotta be fucking kidding me?"

"You owe me sixty bucks, fresh meat. Pay up."

Kierra rolled her eyes and mumbled around the gag, not that they could understand her. "Fucking idiots."

Kenny turned and headed out of the bedroom. Asif waved amiably at her – as if he hadn't kidnapped her and tied her to a chair – and followed him into the hallway. He closed the door behind him.

Kierra listened for the sound of their footsteps down the hall and descending the ancient and thankfully creaky staircase. She waited for the sound of the door to the kitchen closing shut. Then she counted to fifty, working slowly to loosen the bedsheet around her wrists and slip from the bindings. She'd kept her wrists flexed as Kenny wound the fabric together and prayed that he wasn't experienced enough to know that that would matter. At fifty, she was still working to untie her left ankle when she heard the front door open. Kierra froze and listened to the heavy footfalls of whoever had entered. They didn't climb the stairs.

She finally undid the tight knot around her ankle. She ripped the gag out of her mouth and stepped slowly out of the bedroom, stopping to listen. She slowly inched to the landing at the top of the stairs and stopped again, ready to hide in one of the other bedrooms. But all she heard was the endless settling of an old house in need of many repairs.

pink slip

Kierra stepped gingerly down the stairs, her back grazing the wall where she knew the stairs were less likely to creak. She held her breath the entire way.

She turned the knob to the front door and pulled it open slowly, her eyes trained behind her, just in case someone appeared in the hallway. When the door was open just enough for her to slip through, she did. She was just about to take off running when a very familiar sound made her heart stop.

"Now where are you going, sweet girl?"

She jumped and turned toward Lane's voice just as the front door was wrenched open, the house's entrance framing Monica's tall, strong body and hard, angry face. Kierra's mind replayed everything that had happened in the span of no more than thirty minutes and she belatedly put two and three together. She glared at Lane, because when Monica's face was bunched up in that way, Kierra knew she wasn't inclined to answer any questions. "What the hell is going on here?"

That same easy smile that made every atom in Kierra's body sing with electricity spread even wider across his face.

"We missed you too."

Monica

Monica was pacing. She didn't normally pace, she considered it a tell. And she hated tells. They were a liability in her line of work and in her personal life. She didn't like for anyone to know how she was feeling or what she was thinking until she was ready to tell them. After over twenty years, she had become accustomed to Lane's almost preternatural ability to either discern her moods or to tease her into revealing herself. But Kierra was even more gifted. She had gotten under her skin from the moment they met and had stayed there. The realization was just as jarring today as it had been three years ago.

There had been a moment in Serbia where Monica had allowed herself to be deluded into believing that letting Kierra inside would be okay for just a little while. That she could let her guard down and when the time came, put her shields back up. When she'd finally had a taste, literally and figuratively, she'd thought she could close Kierra away in a box and move on. But that fantasy had quickly evaporated, and Monica had come to her senses.

Kierra wanted to be a poet. She was smart and funny and wore her heart and her lust on her sleeve. Monica loved all of that, but she loved it all with the knowledge that she couldn't have it. She and Lane couldn't have Kierra. Because they would ruin it. They would ruin her. Their life was dangerous. And Kierra was a liability. Her leaving was the right decision, but Monica's heart was still aching.

She never should have let her in.

They were all crowded into a barely modern kitchen in a near dilapidated old house in the Irish countryside, a Serbian operative tied to a kitchen chair, gagged and unconscious in front of them. But all Monica could think about was the soft floral scent of Kierra's perfume wafting toward her in the cramped room.

Monica heard Kenny's voice in the foyer. "Thank you so much for your participation these last few days. We appreciate your work. I think you'll find a nice bonus in your pay envelope as a token of our appreciation."

Kierra rolled her eyes and clucked her tongue. "I want my money back for the retreat I was *supposed* to be at," she said to Lane. "And you're getting me admitted again next year."

Monica's spine straightened, but she bit back her own reply.

Lane's voice was easy, nonchalant. "Anything you want, sweet girl."

"Don't call me that," Kierra yelled. She turned to Monica then and said, "You don't get to call me that anymore."

Monica opened her mouth, unsure of what she was about to say, but feeling an intense urge to say something, anything. But words came so hard for her. And then Kenny strolled into the kitchen.

"Alright," he said with a clap of his hands. "Did I miss the interrogation?

None of them responded. Monica was staring at Kierra who was staring back in a way she never normally did; with a challenge in her eyes. Until Asif walked into the kitchen from the basement and Monica saw in Kierra's eyes what she'd missed before: fear.

"Did he hurt you?" Monica asked, nodding her head to the unconscious man tied up between them.

"No," Kierra ground out.

Monica noted, but did not acknowledge, the fact that Kenny and Asif had gone particularly still, and Lane had shifted into a ready stance.

"Who?" Monica asked.

Kierra's eyes darted to Asif and then back.

"Did *he* hurt you?"

Kierra bit her bottom lip and her right hand unconsciously grabbed her left wrist.

"Okay, wait. I can explain," Kenny yelled, his hands flying up, just as Lane pulled a Glock from a holster underneath his jacket and aimed it directly at Kenny's temple.

Monica kept her eyes on Kierra, who was keeping a wary eye on Asif who stood, certainly not by accident, behind Monica.

"Do you trust them?" Kierra asked.

"We don't trust anyone," Monica said. And then after a second of hesitation, "Except you."

Kierra's eyes began to thaw and Monica tried not to glory at the conflict on her face, indicating that there was still some hope but that she was not ready not to be mad at all of them.

"You sent them here to watch me?"

"To watch out for you," Lane clarified.

"Did you tell them to tie me up?"

That was when Monica saw the hurt that the fear was hiding. "Absolutely not," she said. "Who tied you up?" The question was a demand and a threat.

Kierra never got to answer.

"I only helped because he fucking forgot his accent and grabbed her," Kenny said, his voice pleading.

Monica turned slowly to Asif.

"She was freaking out," Asif said in his thick Boston accent with his charming grin, which might have worked if Monica had been willing to be charmed.

"So you tied her up?" Lane asked, keeping his eyes on Kenny.

"It seemed like a good idea at the time," Asif replied, far too casually for Monica's liking.

If he was going to say any more, they would have to wait until he woke up. Monica punched him in his jaw and his head whipped to the right. He was unconscious before his body hit the dingy laminate floor. She turned back to Kierra. Monica's hand hurt, her heart was racing and she was taking deep breaths into her nose and releasing them out of her mouth, trying desperately to calm herself down.

Monica was dangerous, but she didn't relish violence. She did her job because she believed in it. But as her eyes locked on Kierra's and scanned her face, she catalogued her former PA's response to watching her punch out the man who'd ordered her tied up, a man she worked with. Without hesitation. Kierra's eyes were dilated, her nostrils flared and her mouth parted in surprise and lust. Monica wondered, if she moved her eyes, would she be able to see Kierra's hard nipples through her thin t-shirt? And then her mind wandered, and she couldn't help but wonder if she took those few steps separating them and touched her, the way she wanted to, would her skin be warm? Would her pussy be wet? And she realized that she would fight the world if it made Kierra feel safe.

"Him too?" Monica asked. Kenny whimpered. The question was layered. Had Kenny tied her up? Did Kierra want Monica to punch Kenny as well? Did she want Lane to shoot him? Would that be enough to apologize for putting her in danger? For letting her leave Serbia without them?

Monica was just about to ask all of those questions and more. And she could see that Kierra's body was turning on the point of expectation, just waiting. And she knew where that would lead; exactly where it shouldn't. And she was making her peace with that when Lane's voice cut through the moment.

"Serbian's waking up," he announced. He holstered his gun and said in a dark voice to Kenny, "We'll finish this later."

Lane walked to stand next to Monica, putting his hand on the small of her back, anchoring her in reality and what they had to do. Monica resisted for a second but then dropped her eyes.

"You shouldn't be here for this, sw-," he hesitated and then finished, "Why don't you go to the library, Kierra? Just don't leave the house."

"No," Kierra said in a defiant voice. "This is all about me, right? So I'm staying."

Lane opened his mouth to argue with her, but Monica cut him off.

"Okay," she said and then turned to her husband. "She's right. She should stay."

"Are you sure?" He asked yet another layered question.

And the answer was no, she wasn't. She'd been arguing for three years that it was best to keep Kierra at bay; as far away from the mess of their lives as possible. That was the right thing to do. Her stance on that hadn't changed. But the flash of anger she felt at their mission and at Asif for tying Kierra up and Kenny for allowing it and herself for not being there when the Serbian operative had made his move felt all-consuming. Because Serbia had destabilized her resolve.

Kierra's laugh and the way she rolled her eyes and gasped Lane's name when he was inside her and her mouth trailing soft kisses up Monica's back. All of that had slithered under Monica's skin. Kierra had sunk almost as deep into her bones as Lane and she realized that the last three months without her had been torture. Because she had been right all along. Kierra was a liability. And Monica was completely compromised.

thirteen

Kierra was great at multi-tasking. She always had been. But right now her skills were being tested. She was currently moving around the tiny kitchen trying to dodge the spray of blood and sweat flinging from Monica's hands as she beat the Serbian operative to a pulp in front of her. She was also trying to stay as far away from Kenny, who was splitting his time between looking at her with sad, apologetic eyes, that she ignored, and trying to rouse Asif awake. Although Kierra appreciated that Kenny seemed to be hitting Asif far harder than was necessary.

She was also avoiding Lane, who had taken up a position behind Monica and was using a very large knife to pretend to clean his fingernails. Kierra knew it was an act because she'd personally booked Lane's manicures for three years. But a large knife was a large knife when you were trying to scare an assassin.

She was also trying to process the lengths to which her former bosses had gone to protect her, even if she didn't yet know from what. And she was trying to do all of that while pointedly not remembering the wild lust in Monica's eyes after she'd punched Asif. Kierra's body had shivered at the danger of Monica's whispered, "Him too?" If Lane hadn't interrupted them, she wasn't sure what she'd have said, but she knew exactly what she'd wanted to do.

The Serbian groaned and began to yell in English, "Stop. Stop. I tell you."

Kierra shook herself back to reality and made a mental note that she needed to talk to her therapist when she got home.

"Wonderful," Lane announced, replacing Monica in front of their hostage, that big easy smile on his face. Monica moved to the kitchen sink and began to rinse off her bloody hands.

"Hand me that chair, sweet girl. I mean… Kierra," Lane said.

It was pure habit that she'd already reached for a chair before he'd fully formed the request on his lips. And it was because the room was so small that Kierra had to brush along Monica's body to hand the chair to him. Or at least that's what she told herself. She also accepted that the slightest brush of Monica's hand on her hip must have been a figment of her imagination.

"Do you three want to be alone?" Kenny asked the question and shrunk back when Monica turned to glare at him. "Never mind."

"Now," Lane said, lowering his lanky body into the chair, "Let's get down to business." And then he proceeded to interrogate the Serbian in Serbian.

"Hold up," Kierra yelled and everyone in the room, including the Serbian, excluding a still unconscious Asif, turned to her. "How am I supposed to understand if you're talking in Serbian?"

She heard Kenny scoff and pretend it was a cough as Monica shifted toward him. But Lane kept his eyes on her and an amused grin on his face.

"He doesn't speak enough English. Maybe Monica can translate for you," he said simply and then turned back to the operative.

Monica's body shifted closer to Kierra's side and she shivered. It was yet another absurd moment. Kierra was standing in the middle of this ugly kitchen, not at the writing retreat she'd paid thousands of dollars to attend, with five people who could certainly kill her with one hand, so horny she could feel sweat dripping down her back.

She turned to Monica. The question was in her eyes. She could see it because that had been her job: to decipher and anticipate all of Monica's needs and questions and then act accordingly. And three months ago she would have nodded and let Monica lean into her body and whisper the translation against her ear and cheek and neck. And after Serbia there was a chance that Monica would have let her tongue trail along Kierra's skin in the wake of the translated words. Kierra would have squirmed, rubbing her thighs together, full to bursting with all that she needed and wanted. But that was before they'd stood in a stairwell, Kierra practically begging them to ask her to stay, and they'd let her go. Her eyes locked with Monica's and she didn't nod, she only stared back in challenge. If Monica wanted to translate for her, if she wanted to get that close to her ever again, she'd have to ask.

Asif moaned.

"He's awake," Kenny announced. "Almost."

"Of course he's awake. If she'd wanted to kill him, she would have," Lane said, affronted on Monica's behalf.

"Get him out of here," Monica demanded, her eyes on Kierra but the command for Kenny.

"I'll help," Kierra said, moving around Monica to help Kenny pull Asif to his feet.

"I thought you said you wanted to be here for this?" Lane asked the question, his body turned around in his chair to see her. Monica turned around slowly, her eyes trained on Asif's face, even though Kierra knew that she was waiting for her answer.

Kierra sighed and shook her head. "You can tell me everything, and I mean everything, after."

She and Kenny struggled to haul Asif into the library. Once inside, they both dumped him unceremoniously facedown onto a couch.

"Huh, I guess he's still passed out," Kenny said.

"Good," Kierra breathed, moving toward the window and pulling back the curtains to peer out into the afternoon sun, such as it was behind all the gray cloud cover.

Kenny ran to her, "Actually, let's keep those closed," he said and pulled the curtains shut.

"Why?"

"Because."

"What's going on here?"

"It's not my place to tell you that. You should wait for Monica and Lane."

Kierra's eyes brightened and she changed her line of questioning. "Are those really their names or just a cover? Is Kenny really your name? Asif?"

"Don't tell her that," Mrs. Wilde said, walking into the room. She stopped and looked at Asif's prone body, shrugged and refocused on Kenny. "Don't tell her anything."

Kierra rolled her eyes. "You can drop the Irish accent. I know you're all spies."

Mrs. Wilde looked at her with a bland frown and she said, in a seemingly thicker Irish accent than before, "I'm not a spy and I'm not a cook. But I *am* Irish." She turned to Kenny. "But you are a spy. Have a bit more of a backbone, will you."

Kenny's back straightened. "I wasn't going to tell her anything," he said defensively.

Mrs. Wilde eyed them both skeptically before turning to walk out of the library as quickly as she'd entered.

"I don't like her," Kierra announced.

"I agree." Kenny turned to her. "So what's up with you and them?"

Kierra shook her head. "That's none of your business." She walked past him and collapsed into a chair.

Kenny stayed at the window.

The house was silent now. Whatever intel the Serbian was giving up down the hall, they couldn't hear it. All Kierra could hear was the endless settling of the house. She reached into her back pocket and pulled out her cellphone. She chewed her bottom lip, considered her wording and then started typing out a text message to Maya.

"What are you doing?" Kenny almost screeched.

"Texting my roommate," Kierra replied glibly.

"Don't do that," he said, his hand coming over her shoulder, reaching for her phone.

Kierra jumped out of her seat and moved across the sitting area; her phone clutched in her hand. "Hands off. You've done enough damage today."

Kenny at least had the decency to look embarrassed. "Okay, I shouldn't have let Asif tie you up."

"You also tied me up," she countered.

He put his hands up in surrender. "Okay, we made a mistake. But you were freaking out and we needed to keep you in the house. We don't know if the guy in the kitchen is alone or not."

There was something about the way Kenny spoke that made the lightbulb go off in her head. "You're new, aren't you?"

He seemed to bristle at the question. "What makes you say that?"

Kierra shrugged. It was difficult to explain. Through Monica and Lane, she'd met a few other spies, or at least people she reasonably assumed were spies, and they'd all seemed confident and sure in their actions in a way Kenny definitely did not. She thought about saying that, but considering the way he'd stiffened at her questions, she wasn't sure that would get her the answer she wanted. She shrugged instead. "Just a thought."

He considered her for a second and, she thought, was about to answer, when Asif started moaning again. Kenny's eyes darted to him. When he looked back, his gaze was shuttered.

Kierra exhaled loudly and turned to Asif. "Dick," she said to his back.

They watched Asif return to consciousness. He sat up on the couch, rubbed his eyes and then gingerly touched his jaw. When his eyes landed on Kierra, she gave him a smug smile. He smiled, winced and then shrugged.

There was a flurry of activity down the hall and they all turned toward it. Kierra walked to the door and peered around the wall, trying to see. And then Kenny and Asif's large bodies tried to crowd into the doorway as well. They were jostling for positions like children on timeout. It was very embarrassing. But when they spotted Monica and Lane seemingly having an argument down the hall, they quieted down to eavesdrop. Kierra had never seen them argue.

"That's a bad idea," Lane said to Monica who was passing in and out of sight from the hallway to the front door, pacing. Another thing Kierra noted she'd never seen Monica do before today.

"It's our only option," she ground out.

"It's not and you know it." Lane stepped in front of Monica and reached out to grasp her upper arms. "We could just tell her."

Kierra felt her face warm at his words and because Kenny and Asif had turned toward her. For a second, her only wish was to crawl into a hole and hide, and then she got angry. She stepped into the hallway. Kenny reached out, trying to pull her back but she skirted his hands and began to walk down the hall to her former employers. They turned toward her and watched.

Kierra wished she had packed for this possibility. She was just in a pair of skinny jeans and a t-shirt. If she'd had her choice, she'd have been wearing some barely appropriate short dress and high-heeled strappy sandals for this moment. But as their eyes traveled up and down her body appreciatively, she realized that she might as well have been naked for all they cared. She'd missed that. The way she always felt sexy and powerful with their eyes on her, undressing her piece by piece.

Lane

Lane watched Kierra walk down the hallway toward them, suddenly reminded of her first day at work. It was a memory that he and Monica revisited a lot while having sex, especially during the last three months, when their longing for her had reached a fever pitch.

She'd shown up for work almost an hour early, eager, caffeinated and wearing a dress tighter than he might have recommended for a first day at a new job. But since her ass looked great in it, neither he nor Monica bothered to mention it. They'd just walked her around their decoy office on the first floor of their home trying not to ogle her as obviously as they clearly wanted.

She'd been so clueless then; she absolutely was not now. But that wasn't what brought the memory to the fore. It was the way Monica's breath hitched as Kierra drew closer to them with confident strides. Lane had always loved the way Kierra set Monica on edge with just a glance or a smile or a laugh. Even he had to work hard to undo her hard façade, so he always appreciated that Kierra was his own personal shortcut to glimpse the churning heat that lived just under Monica's surface. It was an inconvenient thought at a moment like this, but when had their lust ever been appropriately timed?

"You owe me an explanation," Kierra said, when she was just a few feet away.

"It's too dangerous," Monica replied quickly.

"She has a right to know," Lane said. Monica turned to glare at him. He shrugged.

"Tell me. Please," Kierra said.

Lane watched Monica's eyes close. He realized that she would give in. Not because he was right, and Kierra did deserve to know why her life was in danger. But because if she'd once been able to deny the attraction between them, that resolve had been abandoned in a Serbian villa in a haze of lavender-scented body oil and a bed just big enough for the three of them. But also because Kierra's normally confident voice that sounded like ringing bells and went straight to his gut and his dick, had turned the word "please" into a mournful sigh that broke something in Lane. When he turned to Monica, he saw that it had had the same effect on her as well.

She turned back to Kierra and nodded. "Let's go to your room." Monica turned to walk up the stairs. Kierra followed immediately. Lane walked behind them up the stairs, trying to keep his eyes from drifting down her body.

He failed.

***

In Kierra's room, Monica shivered at the draft.

"It's cold in here," Lane said.

"I know. You couldn't have found a better place to stash me?" Kierra said as she sat on her rumpled bed.

He gave her an apologetic grin. "We were in a bit of a hurry. But we'll make it up to you." He said the last sentence with raised eyebrows and the dirty grin that always made Monica consider giving him exactly what he wanted when he wanted. She never did, but he could always make her consider it.

"No," Monica said in a hard tone. Lane turned to her, his eyes dancing. Kierra tried to hide the small movement, but Lane clearly saw her rub her thighs together in his peripheral vision. And with the way her eyes dilated, he guessed Monica had noticed the movement as well.

"This is serious. No flirting," she said to Lane. And she turned to Kierra, "And no..." But she didn't know how to finish the sentence because Kierra didn't flirt per se. Maybe if she did, Monica would have known better how to handle her. "No doing that thing you do," she finished lamely.

Lane wanted to chuckle, but he pressed his lips together, not wanting to interrupt their flow. He enjoyed the way Kierra challenged Monica, pressing her to emote and be more open.

Kierra leaned back on her hands so that her breasts jutted forward. She kept her knees together.

"That," Monica said. "None of that either."

Lane at least had the decency to cover his mouth with his hand, even though the movement barely muffled his laughter.

Monica rolled her eyes. "Can we- You said you wanted to know what's going on. Can we get to that?"

Kierra seemed to deflate at the reminder that she was in danger. Monica waited for her to compose herself before she began.

"Do you remember Banovíc's minister of finance?"

"Martin Stepanov," Kierra replied dutifully. Lane tried to ignore the itch at the back of his throat.

"Apparently, he has not taken Banovíc's death well."

Kierra's eyes widened. "He sent that man after me?"

"He's sent a few men after you actually," Lane breathed. "We've been running interference for months."

Suddenly Kierra's mind flashed back to all those strange moments that made the hair on her arms stand up. "There was someone watching me at the airport," she said.

"He's downstairs," Monica's announced. "We've been tracking him for a while, verifying that he was alone and then trying to figure out where his orders are coming from."

"And that car crash a few months ago?"

Lane smiled, "Yeah, but that wasn't us. We were running down some leads in Berlin and sent those two idiots downstairs to watch after you. Their team is not nearly as discreet as we'd hoped. You wouldn't have noticed anything at all if we'd been there."

Kierra chewed her bottom lip and bent over to drop her head into her hands, clearly trying to process this all.

"We won't let Stepanov get to you," Monica said in a fierce whisper. "We would have handled him long before now, but he's gone into hiding."

Kierra raised her eyes to look at her. "He's not taking over for Banovíc?"

Monica shook her head and Lane answered. "We assumed that he would make a power grab or suck up to whoever did. We honestly didn't expect him to go to these lengths for revenge."

"But why me?" Kierra asked, her voice turning high-pitched with fear. "All I did was walk around damn near naked. You two killed his friend."

Lane watched Monica walk across the room and kneel in front of Kierra. She grasped her hands and looked her deep in the eyes. Lane might have given her platitudes and consoled her that everything would be okay. But Monica wasn't good at that. She turned to him, her eyes beseeching him to tell Kierra what she couldn't.

"Tell me," Kierra begged as if she understood Monica's dilemma.

"You should have been able to slip out of the country unnoticed," Monica said. "That's why we split up. If we'd all left together, there was a chance that we might have stuck out."

"Three foreigners who can't keep their hands off each other. Not too inconspicuous," Lane interjected.

"The only person who knew when you left and where from besides us was our chauffeur. He was part of a rogue faction within Serbian intelligence."

"He betrayed us?" Kierra gasped.

"Only after a significant amount of torture," Monica said simply. "And they killed him anyway."

"So he's trying to kill me?"

"Eventually, yes. But right now we think he's trying to draw us out. And we're trying to draw him out. That's why we needed to get you somewhere isolated. Fewer surprises this way," Lane said.

Kierra licked her lips. Lane allowed himself to savor the sight of her pink tongue and wet lips.

"Did the guy downstairs give you anything useful?"

Lane laughed as he moved behind Monica who was still crouching at her feet. He put his hands over hers and leaned down to bring his face close to Kierra's. He heard Monica's movements as his lips got dangerously close to Kierra's; the potential for relief near but far away.

"How about one more mission, sweet girl?"

Monica wanted Kierra to say no, Lane could feel the tension in her body. They never should have dragged her into this in the first place. But more than anything Lane wanted her to say yes. He knew that if he could keep Kierra close, he could keep her safe. The problem would be letting her go once the mission was complete. She'd done it once, but neither of them was sure she could do it again.

fourteen

Kierra was trying not to squirm. But the sounds of Monica and Lane's mission voices (direct, hard, and demanding) were doing something to her that she hadn't felt in a while. Three months to be exact. Something familiar and very unwelcome, since they were on a plane to Berlin hoping to draw the corrupt Serbian politician trying to kill her out of hiding. But still, those voices were washing over her, seeping into her skin like water on dry, cracked earth. Also, the supple leather of the seat against her bare legs was like sensory overload.

Maybe the thin, short, flirty summer dress she'd thrown on for the trip had been a mistake. But when she'd gone to pack her bags to leave the drafty old house that had tormented her for three days, she hadn't been thinking about wearing practical mission attire. She'd been thinking the same thing she always did when she dressed for the Peters: what would draw Monica and Lane's eyes and maybe even their hands to her.

Old habits die hard.

"Okay, that's enough for now. We'll regroup in Berlin," Lane said, clapping his hands together.

"Will your contact show?" Monica asked Asif the question with a slight sneer in her voice. Kierra tried not to gloat, but she was still on cloud nine that Monica had knocked him out cold. For her.

"She'll be there," he said simply, absently rubbing at his jaw.

Monica dismissed him with a curt nod and turned to lock eyes with Kierra. "Can we talk to you?" She tilted her head toward the back of the plane. Where the bedroom was.

Kierra knew she should say no. She should say that whatever they had to say, they could say out here in front of

Kenny and Asif. That the three of them being near a bed, especially in a small room that was only big enough for the bed itself, was a very bad idea. But the list of all the things she should say only popped into her brain when she had already squeezed between Monica and Lane's bodies on either side of the aisle and shivered as her bare arms made the slightest contact with Lane's broad chest and Monica's hard biceps. And by that point, she rationalized to herself, it was probably too late to turn back. So she lifted her head slightly and strode confidently, excitedly, toward her own personal ruin.

Old habits, blah blah blah.

There was nowhere else to sit but on the bed. She crossed her legs, the dress's short skirt skimming very high on her thighs. She'd assumed that Monica and Lane would sit next to her, but they stood instead, their backs against the door, their tall bodies looming over her. Kierra sucked her bottom lip into her mouth and tried very hard not to think about all the times she'd dreamt of being in just this position, or of that one time she was.

"Well?" She said, lifting her chin, hoping that she seemed annoyed rather than too aroused to breath more than that one word.

"We wanted to talk to you about Berlin," Monica said carefully.

"Didn't you just brief us on Berlin for like an hour?"

"That was about the mission. This is about us," Lane said.

It was an innocuous couple of sentences but something about them sent Kierra over the edge. She stood up quickly and pointed a finger at them both. "There is no us. You let me leave Serbia by myself."

"It was the best way to keep you safe, Kierra," Monica said, her voice gritty, as if she was trying to restrain herself. Kierra had never heard her sound quite like that.

"And then you didn't call me or anything for *three months.*"

"We were busy trying to keep you alive," Lane said, his voice still affable, but frayed. A very big difference from his regular light and easy tone.

"And would that have been easier or harder if you'd just told me what was happening?"

Lane laughed and Kierra swiveled her neck back in shock.

"Knowing you," he said, putting his hands on his hips as if he were so exasperated by her, "it would have been harder."

"We thought about telling you," Monica said, "but you wanted to move on, and we wanted to respect that."

"No, I wanted to stay. And I told you that. It was you two who didn't want to be with me anymore." Kierra took a deep breath in and tried not to cry even though the pressure behind her eyes was building.

"If we'd have told you, we'd have had to stash you away somewhere. Away from your friends and your life."

An angry tear fell down Kierra's face. "Would I have been with you?" She asked in a small voice, even though the question made her feel foolish.

"Yes," Monica replied immediately.

Kierra refused to give them the satisfaction of knowing how that answer soothed her. She swiped at the wet trail across her cheek.

"And that would have been a problem," Lane added gently.

"Why?"

He laughed ruefully. "I don't know how to tell you this, sweet girl, but you're a big fucking distraction for us. And we can't be hiding away in a hotel room fucking ourselves into a stupor if we want to find Stepanov and put an end to this."

Kierra understood that he was right. But she also heard Monica's sharp intake of breath when Lane said 'fucking' and then she felt moisture pool at her core. Her body was a hormonal mess when she was near them, which made her consider that maybe he had a point.

Lane shook his head and laughed softly. "See. You two can't even be angry at each other without getting wet."

Kierra's face warmed and she snuck a peek at Monica, who leaned into Lane's side but kept her eyes on Kierra, her mouth parted slightly.

Kierra lifted her eyes to Lane's, still defiant. "Well, if I'm such a liability, why are you taking me to Berlin?"

"Two reasons," Lane answered. "First, we already know Stepanov wants to get to us through you. So if we all show up together, it should draw him out."

Kierra nodded. That had been the crux of the hour-long briefing, so basically it could have been two minutes, she thought and crossed her arms in annoyance.

"Second," Lane began, but Monica finished.

"We missed you."

Kierra lifted an eyebrow at Monica and said in her hardest tone, which wasn't even a fraction of the steel that Monica could muster, "Prove it."

Monica pushed away from the door and would have tackled Kierra to the bed, but Kierra put out a hand to stop her. She had never felt so powerful. Her one slim index finger stopping Monica Peters mid-step. After three years of feeling as if she was caught up in the maelstrom of her own lust, Kierra could hardly breath with that kind of control literally at her fingertips. She shook her head and walked Monica back to the door, that index finger between them, just barely, but not quite, touching Monica in the center of her chest. Lane grunted his approval.

Kierra kept moving forward, skimming that finger lightly along Monica's angular jaw and pressed her body to Monica's front. She had to bite her lips to stop from moaning as Monica's hands grasped her bare thighs. Her fingers dug possessively into Kierra's flesh.

Apparently, she actually had been missed.

She let Monica knead her legs, slipping just under her dress briefly, before reaching down to push her hands away.

"I wanted to stay with you." She whispered the words against Monica's lips. "I would have begged, if you'd let me."

"Kierra," Monica moaned.

Kierra cut off Monica's words with a sharp shake of her head. "If you want to show me that you missed me, then you do it on my terms."

"And your terms are?" Lane asked, an amused lilt in his voice.

Kierra rubbed herself against Monica and lightly brushed her mouth against her lips. Monica's lips parted and she leaned forward, but Kierra backed away. "You don't touch me until I say so."

Lane grunted. Kierra smiled and turned toward him. "But if there's something you want to do to me, you can do it to each other." She turned back to Monica and traced her tongue along the seam of the other woman's lips. "While I watch."

Monica's eyes were dilated and bored into Kierra's. If there had ever been a moment since Serbia where Kierra had thought that Monica didn't care for her, that they had used her for their own pleasure – and there had – there was no way that Kierra could entertain those thoughts again. Not when Monica was looking at her as if she was the sun.

Good, Kierra thought to herself, now she knows how I felt these last three years. Kierra moved back from Monica's body and missed the contact immediately. She raised an eyebrow and Monica moved to the side, pulling the door open for Kierra to walk through. And she did, rubbing her body along Monica's one last time for good measure.

"A goddamn distraction," Lane said, his amused chuckle following Kierra down the aisle.

***

"Where's Asif?" Kierra asked Kenny, plopping down in the seat across from him.

"Calling his favorite asset to make sure she's on her way to Berlin," he replied, a smile arcing across his lips, as he tapped at his cell phone.

"Favorite?"

Kenny raised his eyes at the question. "Great thief, questionable morals, loves to flirt." He tilted his head to consider her. "Actually, you two would probably get along."

Kierra scoffed. "I don't steal," she said.

He smiled. "Neither does she. She calls her heists inanimate liberations," he said and rolled his eyes before returning his attention to his phone.

"Who are you texting?" She asked, leaning slightly forward as if to see his phone.

He clutched his phone to his chest. "None of your business."

"Sorry, I'm nosy."

"We're spies. We're all nosy. The trick is to not be too nosy with the people you work with."

"One," Kierra said raising her index finger, "I'm not a spy. And two," she raised her middle finger, "you should absolutely be nosy about the other people you work with if they're also spies. That's just common sense."

"She's got a point," Asif said, moving down the aisle to sit with them. Annoyingly, he sat next to Kierra and leaned toward her. "No wonder they like you so much."

Kierra turned toward him with a hard stare. "I don't think Monica would like you being this close to me." At the mention of Monica's name, Asif's smile fell away and he moved to sit next to Kenny instead. Kenny watched Asif scurry across the aisle with a broad smile on his face and Kierra winked at him.

"Why aren't you mad at him?" Asif whined, pushing Kenny's elbow from the armrest between them. "We both tied you up. Besides, you hated him at the retreat."

Kierra aimed a pained smile at Kenny who shrugged in return.

"It was the mission," he said blithely. "No hard feelings."

"He was following orders. And I thought I could trust you."

Asif shrugged, "Don't trust anyone. That's my advice."

"I didn't ask for your advice," Kierra said.

"Okay, let's change the subject," Kenny cut in.

"Yes, let's," Asif responded. "What's with you and Mr. & Mrs. Smith?"

Kierra's face warmed. "I was their PA," she said, as if that answered his question.

"Do PAs normally fuck their bosses or did they have to negotiate your salary for that? And do you need a new job?"

Kierra saw red and opened her mouth ready to bite Asif's head off, but Kenny beat her to it. He stood up quickly and pulled Asif up by his shirt collar. "It's not your place to ask her about her sex life. Apologize."

Asif had a small smirk on his face and Kierra was worried that he would resist and then they would start fighting. She was lifting out of her chair to get out of the line of fire when Asif's voice caught her off guard. "I apologize," he said, his eyes locked with Kenny's. "I didn't mean any disrespect."

Kenny let him go and moved away from them down the aisle, his steps tense and jerking with rage. Asif turned to Kierra; his face contrite. "Honestly, some of my best friends are sex workers," he said around a laugh.

Kierra rolled her eyes at him. "I liked you better with the fake Irish accent."

Asif shrugged, "You wouldn't be the first person to tell me that."

"We got a problem here?" Lane yelled down the aisle as he and Monica approached.

Asif put his hands up quickly. "No problem. Just talking."

Monica stopped in the aisle and looked down at Kierra. "Are you okay?"

Kierra licked her lips and nodded.

pink slip

Monica nodded once, turned to Asif, who flinched, and sat down across the aisle from them.

***

Kierra fell asleep in the car on the way to the Agency safe house.

Monica roused her almost awake when they arrived with a gentle hand on her cheek. Kierra unconsciously rubbed her face into the palm of Monica's hand. She'd missed her touch desperately. But then she remembered her own rules and startled fully awake.

Monica's eyes were amused and aroused but she moved her hand. "We're here."

The safe house was actually more of a compound disguised as an American suburb on the outskirts of Berlin. It was an odd base, hidden in plain sight. As she walked from the car to the front door, she looked up and down the street. It seemed as if the townhomes were occupied – cars parked on the street or in driveways – but the night was a little too dark, too quiet. Kierra had the feeling that they were completely alone out here, and it made her shiver.

When she walked through the front door Kenny called, "Clear," from the top of the staircase. Kierra moved further into the small living room just off the front door. It was sparsely decorated with a sofa, coffee table and tv on a small, cheap stand but nothing else. No artwork on the wall, no plants – real or otherwise. Nothing to indicate that someone actually lived here. Because of course, no one did. Kierra recognized this unique brand of lived-in sterility from other safe houses she'd visited over the past three years.

Asif was sitting on the couch, an opened laptop computer on the coffee table in front of him. Lane and Monica walked through the front door behind her.

"External cameras are in place," Lane announced to Asif. "Send the feed to me when they're up."

"You got it," Asif announced.

"When will your asset arrive?" Monica asked him.

"She'll be here bright and early tomorrow morning," Asif said.

"We've got a weapons cache in the city," Lane said to Kenny.

Kenny nodded and headed to the front door. "I'm on it. I'll be back before you know it."

"Be careful," Monica said, and Kierra noted the slight wrinkling of her eyes and realized that she was worried about him. That surprised her. In three years she'd never seen Monica worry over anyone besides Lane and her.

"Yes, ma'am," he said with a charming smile Kierra had never seen before and a salute as he breezed back out the front door.

"Surveillance feeds sent," Asif said, slamming the laptop shut. "I'm going to run down some potential intel at a classy little strip club I know. Anyone wanna tag along? The guys at this place are *very* flexible," he said. Kierra rolled her eyes, but twenty-four hours ago that smile might have worked on her. So much had happened in so little time.

"No? All right. Well you," he said, smiling at Kierra as he finished the sentence, "three have a lovely evening. I sure will." He turned and followed Kenny out into the night.

The sound of the front door closing seemed to echo in the dimly lit room. Kierra turned to Monica and Lane. A few minutes ago she'd been asleep, exhausted from the whirlwind of the day. But now her blood was pounding in her ears as three months of built up arousal unfurled slowly, like a languid cat waking up from an afternoon nap.

"Where am I sleeping?"

"There's a room upstairs," Lane said, that easy smile on his face.

"Where are you two sleeping?"

"There's a room upstairs," Lane repeated.

"Good," Kierra breathed, turning toward the staircase. She heard their shoes thumping on the floor behind her. She could feel their eyes running over her body as she ascended the stairs. She couldn't help but turn to see them over one shoulder. Their gazes were hungry. She could relate.

When she walked into the bedroom, she found her suitcase and two small duffel bags that she knew were Monica and Lane's at the foot of the bed. She bypassed them and walked into the bathroom.

Kierra turned to look over her shoulder again. "I need someone to unzip my dress," she said, even though she was perfectly capable of taking it off on her own. Her eyes locked on Lane. "Will you help me?"

"Any time, sweet girl."

He moved forward and reached out toward her. His knuckles grazed the back of her neck. She shivered. Monica moved to stand in front of her.

"Are we allowed to touch you?"

Kierra's lip was clenched between her teeth. The sound of her zipper releasing as Lane's fingers traced the bared skin at her back, lightly – so lightly he could argue that it was an accident – made her nipples harden. She watched Monica watch her dress fall to the floor at their feet. "Do you want to?"

Monica swallowed and croaked, "Yes."

"What do you want to do to me?"

Monica raised her head and reached for Kierra's face, but she shook her head. "Use your words."

Monica let her hand fall back to her side, her fingertips ghosting down Kierra's stomach. She'd let that slide this time, but only because she was so very horny.

"I want to taste you," Monica said.

Kierra smiled wide and leaned up on the balls of her feet to whisper in Monica's ear. "Taste him instead."

They both turned their eyes to Lane, whose ears had gone bright red.

Monica turned her head to Kierra, their mouths close. Kierra thought she would speak and it was probably a good thing that she didn't. Because if Monica had said something in that deep raspy voice that always made Kierra's sex shiver, she might have broken her own rule and let them touch her anywhere they wanted. For as long as they wanted.

Monica moved forward into Lane's waiting arms. They embraced each other and pressed their mouths together. Kierra moved just in time to watch Lane's tongue slip into Monica's mouth and she moaned at the sight.

Kierra walked behind Lane and reached out to run her hand up his back and down Monica's arm. She moved to Monica's back and pressed her breasts against those firm muscles that she'd once spent what felt like hours kissing and licking and kneading in a state of pure bliss. Monica moaned into Lane's mouth.

Kierra rested her cheek on Monica's shoulder, breathing them in after so long apart as she watched their mouths move together. Her hands rubbed Monica's hips, her fingers slipping just under the hem of her t-shirt, scraping her skin. She pressed her mouth to Monica's ear.

"I want to watch you suck him," she whispered loud enough for Lane to hear. He grunted into Monica's mouth.

Monica broke their kiss and turned to look at Kierra. "Kiss me first," she demanded in the hard tone that she knew made Kierra's heart beat faster.

"After," Kierra replied with a smirk.

"Jesus," Lane laughed.

"That's our girl," Monica said, as she lowered herself to her knees in front of him.

Kierra followed her to the floor, still at her back. They both reached up to unzip Lane's pants.

He was unsurprisingly hard and ready. Monica grasped him firmly by the base. Lane moaned. Her tongue swiped across the head, collecting the beaded pre-come there. But then she stopped and turned to Kierra.

"How do you want it? Fast or slow?"

"Do I get a vote?" Lane groaned; his voice tight with arousal.

"No," Monica said firmly, her eyes never leaving Kierra's.

"Slow," Kierra answered as she wrapped her hands around Monica's body and cupped her breasts.

"Anything you want, sweet girl," she said and then slowly lowered her mouth onto Lane's dick.

Kierra leaned forward and whispered against Monica's cheek. "I want it all," she said, lifting her eyes to watch Lane's face. His eyelids were drooping, but he fought to keep them open, to watch them.

Monica hummed around Lane's shaft, her mouth moving up and down at an excruciatingly slow pace. Kierra kept her hands on Monica's breasts, slowly massaging them, rubbing her thumbs over the nipples that were hard enough to jut prominently through her bra and shirt. She'd had a very vivid dream exactly like this once. Reality was better.

"Fuck I'm close," Lane whispered after a while.

Monica began to move her mouth faster. Kierra slipped her hand down Monica's abdomen and into her pants. Her sex was warm and slick and welcomed Kierra's fingers easily. She kept her eyes on Lane's dick disappearing and reappearing between Monica's lips and began to circle her clit.

Kierra had felt many things in the three years she'd worked for Lane and Monica. Sexy, self-assured and capable were high on the list. And during their brief affair in Serbia, she'd added wanted to the pile. But as Monica sucked Lane to his release and she drove Monica to orgasm, she decided that powerful was also a pretty good descriptor now for sure.

Lane's hands moved to cup the backs of their heads. His hips thrust forward in jerky motions and he came in Monica's mouth.

Kierra slipped another finger into Monica's pussy. She moaned releasing Lane's cock, wet and glistening. And as if he knew exactly what Kierra wanted, Lane turned Monica's face toward Kierra's. Kierra's lips pressed against Monica's, her tongue slipping into her wet mouth. She moaned deep in her throat at the salty taste of Lane's orgasm and she pumped her fingers into Monica's pussy faster. Lane kept a soft pressure behind their heads, not that they needed it. Monica was panting into Kierra's mouth. She kissed and licked at Monica's lips, tasting Lane with every breath. She moved her thumb to circle Monica's clit and she screeched. Kierra had missed that sound. Monica came in a wet gush on Kierra's fingers, her eyes rolling back into her head. Kierra waited for Monica's vision to clear before bringing her fingers to her mouth. She kept her eyes locked to Monica's as she tasted her.

Lane's thumb stroked Kierra's cheek gently. "We really have missed you, sweet girl."

She smiled in return. This didn't heal the wounds of the past three months. But it was certainly a start.

fifteen

Kierra woke up alone. But not in the same way that she'd been alone for the past three months or the three years before that. She had vague memories of Monica and Lane whispering their goodbyes to her, their mouths coming close to her ear and cheek, but not quite touching. The distinctive smell of their bodies mingled on the sheets around her, promising that she was alone, but only momentarily.

The sun was filtering in at the curtain's edges. Even though the room was dark, Kierra could tell that morning had well and truly come. She turned on her back to stare at the ceiling. She considered searching for her cell phone and calling Maya. But if Monica and Lane were right and Stepanov was having her followed and had already made at least two attempts on her life, she didn't want to involve her best friend any more than she already had. Also, how was she supposed to explain the ridiculous turn of events that had brought her to Berlin instead of the mild-mannered Irish writer's retreat she'd paid for?

The reminder that she'd been swindled out of a few thousand dollars by Monica and Lane suddenly pissed her off. She might have had a small nest egg after working for them, but she was still a broke grad student at heart and she made a mental note not to let either of them get anywhere near her again until she had a refund plus a bonus for her troubles deposited into her bank account.

Kierra angrily pulled the covers back on the bed and stood. She walked over to her suitcase, opened it, and pulled out the first shirt and pair of jeans she found. She stomped downstairs to the kitchen barefoot but had to pull up short when she saw a woman in a large t-shirt – her short but toned brown legs bare – dancing around the kitchen to music only she could hear.

"Who are you?" Kierra asked.

The girl jumped slightly and swiveled her head, but when she saw Kierra she smiled and kept dancing. "Morning," she said in that slow Midwestern way that Kierra always associated with her first college roommate. It was not a good association since that girl had had a nervous breakdown after their spring semester midterms, trashed their dorm room and defecated in the communal showers before the paramedics showed up to take her for a psych eval. Kierra sincerely hoped that girl had gotten the help she'd needed, but she was still traumatized from six months of living with her and this stranger's doe-eyed welcome momentarily brought those memories back.

"Who are you?" Kierra asked again.

The girl turned fully around and walked toward her. "You don't remember me?"

Kierra started to shake her head and then gasped, backing out of the kitchen. She had a mental flashback to the day of that strange car accident and the girl who bumped into her and smiled, just like this girl was smiling right now, and the goosebumps she got when she realized that something wasn't right. She also only in that moment realized that there was a knife in the girl's hand. Since she now knew that Stepanov had been aiming to kill her that day, she turned around and ran out of the kitchen, but collided with the large expanse of Kenny's bare chest.

"Ow," he said, stumbling back. "Can you watch where you're going?"

"Kenny, oh my god. There's someone in the kitchen," she hissed.

He reached out immediately to grab her and pulled her behind him, his eyes shifting from lethargic to sharp, which made Kierra realize just how effectively he'd assumed his identity as the most annoying social director ever. They both turned back toward the kitchen just as the girl walked to the threshold, knife in hand.

143

pink slip

"Was it something I said?"

Kenny's body relaxed and he sighed. "Chanté, put the knife down. What is wrong with you?"

"I was making toast," she said innocently. "This was the only knife I could find."

Kenny took two long strides to her and grasped the weapon from her hand. He then turned to Kierra and motioned between them. "Kierra, this is Chanté. She's Asif's asset."

Chanté bounced onto the balls of her feet. "Is that what he calls me?"

"That's what you are," Kenny said.

She leaned into Kenny's side and purred. "It sounds a bit dirty, don't you think?"

Kenny rolled his eyes and moved away from her. "You think everything sounds dirty."

She smiled and turned to Kierra. "That's the only way to live." And then she clapped her hands together. "Who wants toast?" She turned and marched back into the kitchen. "Kenny, bring my knife," she yelled over her shoulder.

Kenny was shaking his head and he looked at Kierra. "She's harmless. She'll flirt with you and she might steal your watch, but that's about it." He gestured for Kierra to follow him into the kitchen, which she did, albeit warily.

If Chanté noticed the tension rolling from Kierra, she didn't seem to care. She flitted from the toaster to the island in the center of the kitchen, expending a great amount of energy presenting the toast to them as if it were a culinary masterpiece. Kenny threw the very large knife in the sink, fished around in a drawer by the stove and pulled out a butter knife. He showed it to Chanté and placed it on the counter next to her.

She smiled at him, "You're an angel, you know that?"

Kenny leaned down so that she could place a soft kiss on his cheek. He tried to hide the smile on his face but couldn't. Kierra wondered for a second at their relationship. And as if

144

Chanté could read her mind, she turned to her and pushed a plate of toast her way.

"Don't get any ideas. Kenny and I are just friends, who happen to get off on loving people we can't have."

"Be quiet, Chanté," Kenny said, his cheeks turning a bright pink, a warning in his tone.

Chanté handed him a plate of toast. "Don't worry, babe. Your secret is safe with me."

"Secrets. Did I just hear my favorite word?" Asif yelled as he walked into the kitchen.

Kierra noted the immediate change in Kenny and Chanté's body language. Kenny took his plate of toast and sat next to Kierra at the island. He kept his eyes low and shoved the dry bread into his mouth, clearly wanting to avoid Asif's attention. And Chanté, who had seemed like a ball of fairy dust come to life – menacingly large knife aside – straightened her back as if she was going to war. Or protecting her heart.

"Mind your business, conman," she said to Asif in a voice that had shifted from Midwestern polite to East Coast jaded.

Asif leaned against the counter next to her. "You always say conman like it's a bad word." He reached out then and lightly touched the hem of Chanté's shirt, which Kierra realized was probably his. "You're always so mean to me." He pretended to pout.

Chanté turned to him then and said in a voice made of steel and frustration, "I treat you the way you want to be treated. You won't let anyone be nice to you without paying a price." The words landed in the middle of the kitchen like an undetonated bomb.

Kierra's gaze fixed on Asif's face. She awaited his answer as if she were watching a telenovela. Asif, who spoke almost incessantly – except for that time when Monica had knocked him out cold –stared back at Chanté with a blank expression.

The front door opened loudly. "Honey, we're home," Lane called out.

The heated moment between Chanté and Asif seemed to break. He moved to the refrigerator, opening it and staring inside, not bothering to actually reach for anything and she turned back to the toaster, her earlier enthusiasm gone as if it never were.

"No," Kierra whispered.

Kenny reached for his second piece of toast. "Don't worry, they'll be back at it again in no time. Those two are a mess over each other," he whispered.

"Really?" Kierra asked, shoving a corner of toast into her mouth.

"Unfortunately."

Kierra could hear Monica and Lane moving toward the kitchen, but she motioned with her hand to keep Kenny talking. His eyes moved to Chanté and then back. "It's not my business to tell. But he doesn't deserve her." He said the last sentence loud enough for Chanté and Asif to hear. Both of their backs stiffened. Monica walked into the kitchen with Lane fast on her heels. Kierra had never been so disappointed to see them.

"Oh great, we're all here," Lane said leaning against the island and grabbing at a piece of toast.

Kierra shot him an angry glare and tried to resist the urge to smile when he furrowed his brows at her in confusion and then winked.

"What'd we miss?"

Kierra shook her head and turned to Monica who pinned her with an intense stare that reminded Kierra of last night, her knees slightly aching from the hard tile on the bathroom floor, Monica's lips around Lane's cock, her pussy pulsing around Kierra's fingers. But then she smiled and the sight of it caught Kierra off guard.

"Good morning," Monica said in a soft voice that was just for her.

"Morning," Kierra croaked back.

"Oh my god, this is so sweet," Chanté said, some of the life coming back to her voice.

Monica's smile faltered but Kierra's didn't. Just knowing that her smile was there, hidden beneath that assessing glare, just waiting to reappear for her made everything else melt away.

Well, almost everything. "You two owe me $3468 for that writing retreat. And I want pain and suffering, but I'll send you a bill for that when this is all over with an exact amount."

Monica frowned and looked at Kierra confused. Lane and Kenny chuckled. Asif finally turned around from the refrigerator, his face returning to the relaxed nonchalance that Kierra recognized, even though he refused to look in Chanté's direction.

And Chanté leaned across the island with a large smile on her face as she stage-whispered, "If Stepanov doesn't kill you, I really hope we can be friends."

Lane

It was a good plan. Lane tried to remind himself of that. It was his plan in any case. But he really wished that it had been Monica's. Lane was a good agent. He was a great agent, actually. But he had no illusions about his character strengths. He didn't lead. He didn't want to lead. Being in charge came to Monica like breathing. It was the thing she'd been born to do. And ever since that night just across the street from campus when he'd been a bit drunk and grateful not to have been robbed of the $16 he had in his pocket – which was actually all the money he had left until payday – he'd been dead set on following her wherever she led. And even with the occasional bullet wound and broken fingers and that one concussion, he'd never regretted it.

Lane desperately wanted to be led in this moment. He'd been waiting for weeks for Monica to see the big picture, come up with a plan and then point him in the direction of implementing it. It was how they normally worked, personally and professionally. But it was only in Ireland that he'd realized that Monica couldn't do that. She hadn't really been able to do that since their last night in Serbia. Losing Kierra had upset her balance and his normally even-tempered and always focused wife suddenly was neither of those things. So for the first time in twenty-three years, it was Lane's turn to step up and chart their way forward. But just this once.

They were all crowded in the living room. Asif, Kenny, Chanté and Kierra were squeezed on the couch like children waiting for a scolding. He and Monica were standing in front of them detailing a ridiculously risky plan. If Monica had designed it, it would have been more cautious. But Monica hadn't and Lane was never more cautious than he had to be.

"This sounds nuts," Kenny said, shooting a skeptical look at Monica as if to say, "You approved this?" Lane could relate.

"It sounds fun," Chanté said.

Lane looked at Asif; the question clear in his gaze, "Is she okay?"

Asif shrugged and rolled his eyes, but his gaze stopped at an angle as he clearly tried to view Chanté in his peripheral vision without being noticed. Lane rolled his eyes. Wonderful, he thought, that's exactly what this mission needs: more emotional entanglements.

As soon as he thought that, Kierra piped up in a small voice that he'd rarely heard. "So basically, the mission is to dangle me in front of Stepanov like fresh meat?"

"Yes," Lane said.

"Like in Serbia?"

"Kinda."

"Exactly," Kierra corrected. "Are all spies one trick ponies or…?" She let the question dangle in a way that Lane knew was meant to get under his skin. Because she loved getting under their skin. The awareness of it made him begin to harden in his pants.

"Later," Monica said, because of course she knew what Kierra was doing and what he was thinking.

"Or now," Chanté offered.

"No please, later," Kenny said, rubbing his forehead. "So basically, you three are gonna go to Stepanov's favorite club and wait for one of his agents to show up?"

"Not one of his agents," Monica said. "Stepanov."

"But he hasn't even been seen in public since Banovíc's funeral. Why would he show up here and now?"

"Because we're here," Lane said matter-of-factly.

"And because we've sent him an invitation," Monica replied.

"Oh yeah, and that."

"What invitation?" Kierra asked, pulling her legs beneath her to sit up taller.

"We had Mrs. Wilde send the agent we caught in Ireland back to Serbia with a message for Stepanov to meet us here if he wanted to find out what really happed to Banovíc," Monica explained. A second later she added, "Well, she sent back parts of him."

Kierra shuddered.

"So, he'll definitely be here," Kenny said.

"He's already here actually," Asif added.

"You've confirmed that?" Lane asked. But Asif turned to Chanté and they all followed his gaze.

She beamed under their attention. "Absolutely confirmed."

"How?" Kierra whispered.

Chanté turned to Kierra, bouncing in her seat. "As it happens, Stepanov and his boyfriend have a standing engagement with a very close and personal friend of mine when they're in town."

Asif grunted and looked away. Chanté ignored him and continued. "They showed up at the club late last night or I guess it was technically early this morning looking for him, but he's in the Netherlands on a tour. They were not happy."

"What kind of club?" Kierra asked.

Lane couldn't see her face, but by the way her voice dropped, and she leaned her shoulder into Kierra's, he knew that Chanté was flirting with her.

"Come by and I'll show you."

Lane could feel Monica's jealousy wafting from her body.

"Sorry, does no one remember that this is a life and death situation?" Kenny asked, pushing up from the couch to pace the room. "Stepanov gets the unnamed body parts of one of his agents telling him to come to Berlin. He arrives in town to avenge his friend's death but the first thing he does is go to a strip club?"

Chanté huffed, "Well now she knows what kind of club it is. Thanks Kenny."

"And a Serbian dictator's bff is trying to kill you," he aimed at Kierra, "But all you can think about is flirting and fucking these two."

Chanté gasped, "So it *is* both of them? I wasn't sure." She turned to Kierra and whispered, "He never tells me anything good." She waved dismissively in Asif's direction.

"That's enough," Lane said in a hard tone. But Kenny ignored him.

"And you two," he turned to Asif and Chanté, "literally just run into each other's lives every few months as if you don't know how dangerous the world is. I mean, what the fuck? Is this really our team?" He aimed the question at Monica.

"Enough," she said in a deadly whisper that seemed to suck all the air out of the room.

Kenny seemed to realize in that moment all he'd said, and his face flushed.

"I'll go check the weapons," he mumbled and walked briskly out of the room.

The living room was silent after his departure for a few seconds until Chanté informed them in her usual bright voice, which Lane had long since learned was a wonderful misdirection and hid how cunning she really was, "Don't mind Kenny. He just really needs to get laid."

Lane turned to Monica, his insecurities about this plan rising by the second. Because maybe Kenny did have a point. Is this really our team, his eyes asked. She nodded at him. If she felt any of his misgivings, she didn't show it. He tried to focus on that. To follow as he always had. Hoping and praying that she wasn't too compromised to protect them from themselves.

sixteen

The rest of the day passed by in the most boring way. Kierra and Chanté bunkered down in the living room to watch German movies with strange English subtitles that never made sense, while the spies flitted past them preparing for tonight's mission. They barely stopped to talk or even acknowledge their presence. Kierra found herself smiling as Chanté rolled her eyes each time someone rushed from one part of the townhouse to another, especially if that someone was Asif.

As the sun began to set, Kenny reappeared from wherever he'd been hiding. He pointed to Kierra, "You need to go get ready." He turned to Chanté, "And I'm supposed to take you to your place and then to work."

Chanté's ever-present smile dipped. "I thought Asif was going to do that?"

Kenny shifted under the question, clearly uncomfortable, but Kierra could tell by his frown and the look in his eyes that what he told her was the truth; he wouldn't lie to spare her feelings and that made Kierra like him immensely. "He said it would be best if I did it."

There was a moment of silent communication between them before Chanté turned to Kierra and hugged her. "See you soon." She bounced up from the couch and grabbed Kenny's arm. "Come on tall, awkward and handsome."

Kenny's sigh made Kierra laugh. When they were gone his earlier words came back to her because he was right. If Chanté's intel was correct and Stepanov was in Berlin, then it was time to get serious. Kierra especially needed to get ahold of herself because it was technically her life on the line; her life that had been on the line for months without her even knowing it. She trudged up to the bedroom on suddenly heavy feet and moved into the bathroom, stripping her clothes off as she went.

She was in the shower, lathering her body, wondering if maybe she should call Maya and remind her that she'd agreed to wipe her hard drive in the event of her death, when there was a knock on the door. Kierra leaned out of the shower and called. "Who is it?"

"Us," Monica said.

Kierra sighed. Maybe she could get her head on straight *after* her shower. "Come in."

The door opened and Monica and Lane walked into the bathroom. Their eyes washed over what little they could see of her body as she peeked around the glass partition. She let them stand there and stare hungrily at her for a second before she cleared her throat.

"Did you two want something?"

Lane expectedly smirked, "You. But that's a given."

Kierra clenched her thighs together out of their line of sight.

"We need you to be ready in an hour," Monica said, her eyes glued to the steamy partition as if willing it to clear so that she could see the rest of Kierra's body.

"You need any help in there?" Lane asked playfully, draping an arm around Monica's waist.

Kierra moved from behind the partition, displaying her wet sudsy self. By this point, putting herself on display for them felt as natural as breathing. Monica absentmindedly licked her lips.

"Have you refunded my money?"

"Is that another condition?" Lane asked.

"Yes. But also, it's only fair."

Monica smirked and they turned and left without another word. Kierra frowned at their backs.

When she'd finished showering, Kierra breezed into the bedroom without a towel, expecting to find Monica and Lane waiting for her. Instead there was a yellow dress on the bed and they were gone. She was disappointed, but the dress helped distract her.

Kierra ran her fingers along the soft fabric and shivered, imagining the way the soft jersey would feel gliding over her skin. She'd just pulled it over her head when Lane walked into the room. He was wearing a gray business suit that accentuated the gray at his temples. He wasn't wearing a tie, so his crisp white shirt was open at the neck. Kierra wanted to lick him there. He wore a thin black belt at the waist, which only accentuated his slim hips and the length of his body, which oddly brought to Kierra's mind the length of his dick.

There was a shoe box in his hands. He stopped to admire the way that the dress hugged her curves. "Monica picked that out," he said, his voice full of pride. It made Kierra's nipples tingle.

"I know," she replied. "If it had been you, I'd just be standing here in a leather thong with studded pasties."

He smiled, but swallowed hard, clearly conjuring that image in his brain. "Not the right look for tonight's club. But maybe another time," he said eventually.

Just then Monica pushed into the room and it was Kierra's turn to swallow the lump in her throat. She was wearing a slightly oversized tuxedo jacket dress that left a lot and a little to the imagination all at the same time. The dress was open at the neck, exposing a large patch of her chest, but the lapels were just high enough that Monica's small breasts unfortunately remained covered. The hem hit her thighs at just the right point to be publicly decent. But Kierra knew that when sitting it would not be nearly as respectable and that made her mouth water. Her light brown legs were shiny, and her ankles looked delicate in her dangerously thin heels. Kierra knew Lane must have picked them. Monica stopped just inside the doorway and let Kierra look. She had a smug grin on her face and Kierra looked away. The room suddenly felt crowded with the three of them and all their lust.

"I brought your shoes," Lane announced.

Kierra turned back to them, attempting to affect a bored look while also struggling not to let her gaze wander to her legs or his Adam's apple. "Did you pick out her shoes?"

"Of course I did," he scoffed.

She turned and moved to the bed, sitting at the foot. Monica sank down next to her, close enough that Kierra could smell the spicy cologne she wore. Monica kept her hands to herself as Kierra had asked. Kierra found that disappointing and arousing at the same time. Lane knelt in front of them and pulled the lid off the box.

Monica leaned into Kierra's side, still not touching, and whispered into her ear, "Do you like your dress?"

"Yes," Kierra croaked.

Lane lifted one strappy open-toed sandal from the box in a shade of yellow that perfectly matched her dress.

"I bought it for you last year," Monica said.

Kierra turned to look at her as Lane lifted one of her feet to slip the shoe on. "Last year?"

Monica's eyes traveled over Kierra's face and she sucked her bottom lip into her mouth.

"Is she wearing any underwear?" Monica asked, her eyes on Kierra but the question clearly for Lane.

"Not a stitch." He buckled the shoe over her ankle and gently placed it back down to the floor. After some rustling, he lifted her other foot.

Monica released her bottom lip and Kierra's eyes locked on it, so close, wet, begging to be sucked into Kierra's mouth.

Lane finished buckling the second shoe and stood.

"Check your bank account," Monica said. "We're leaving in ten."

Kierra watched them walk out of the room, hot and flustered. And wet.

***

155

pink slip

They were in the back of a town car. Asif was driving. Kierra was sandwiched in the backseat between Monica and Lane. Their bodies were close, but still not touching. She was trying to surreptitiously slide her thighs together in frustration. She wondered if maybe she hadn't taken this no touching thing too far.

"We're here," Asif announced, his voice all business.

When the car stopped, Kierra leaned over Lane to look at the club in front of them. The name was written in English, in elegant black lettering on the front of the building: Menagerie.

She sighed, "Do all of these clubs have to have the cheesiest names?"

The bouncer nodded to Lane and pulled the discreet door on the side of the building open as they approached. Kierra followed Monica through and was happy to find that the décor was at least a marked improvement from Club Ménage and Peep.

There were still plush couches along the perimeter, but they were thankfully in a tasteful modern gray and untufted, so the place looked less like a decadent French salon and more like an inviting sitting room. Nothing like the strip club that it actually was.

In fact, Kierra was momentarily surprised to see the stage at the center of the room, with mirrored floors and poles jutting to the ceiling. But when she did notice, she was so mesmerized at all the bodies writhing there that she let Monica and Lane steer her to a couch without registering exactly where they were going.

They positioned her between them and ordered drinks when the cocktail waitress appeared. Kierra's eye flitted from one woman to another but kept coming back to the soft flesh in light brown skin, only slightly darker than Monica's, in front of them. The dancer's tiny thong left absolutely nothing to the imagination from the back and Kierra's eyes danced over her smooth and perfectly round ass as it jiggled in rhythm with the song playing at ear-splitting levels. She smiled in appreciation; that took skill.

When the dancer turned toward them, Kierra's eyes traveled over the front of the bikini and found the shocking pink of it at the cleft of the woman's legs evocative. Her gaze traveled up her gently rounded stomach, to her small and slightly sagging breasts. The outline of her nipples was clearly visible in her bikini top. She was so mesmerized that it took her a while to finally raise her eyes to the dancer's face to realize that she had been practically undressing Chanté with her eyes for a few long minutes. The smirk on Chanté's face indicated that she had very much noticed. Kierra swallowed but didn't look away.

The cocktail waitress returned with their drinks and Lane leaned down to whisper in her ear. She nodded and approached the stage motioning for Chanté.

Chanté smiled big and wide and walked to the curtain at the back of the stage. Just before she disappeared behind it, she turned, locked eyes with Kierra and winked.

"You like her." It wasn't a question and Kierra could hear the jealousy dripping from each of Monica's words.

She turned to her and the look in Monica's eyes confirmed what Kierra heard. She leaned forward and licked the seam of Monica's frown. "Don't worry, boss. I like you more."

Monica shivered and Kierra felt the same surging power pumping through her veins as she had last night.

Lane cleared his throat, reminding them that he was still there. As if they could forget. As if they wanted to. Kierra smiled at Monica and then stood up. She walked in between Lane's spread thighs, straddled him and lowered herself onto his lap, her eyes on Monica the entire time.

His hands moved instinctively to her butt, but she moved them away. She leaned down to press her lips to his. "You're still not allowed to touch me."

pink slip

"For how long?" He asked, the soft texture of his five-o-clock shadow brushing her lips.

She could have said "We'll see," or "I don't know yet," but those would have been lies. They would have seen through them immediately. Because the answer was that her boundaries were clear. She wouldn't let them touch her if they were just going to send her away again as they'd done in Serbia. She'd felt rejected, alone and depressed for months and she wasn't interested in returning to that place again. But Stepanov was still out there, trying to kill them. They all had bigger fish to fry. Kierra weighed the words jumbling in her head, unsure if this was really the right time to have this conversation.

Thankfully Chanté stepped up onto the raised platform where they were seated and interrupted the charged moment between them.

"Well well well," she said in her cheery voice. "Now what do we have here?"

She had thrown a silky robe over herself, but her beautiful legs were still bare, and the robe was hardly tied tight. She slithered into Kierra's abandoned seat.

Monica leaned forward, running an index finger along Chanté's jaw. "Any sign of him?"

Kierra and Chanté were both caught up in the moment. Kierra's eyes on that simple hair's breadth meeting of their skin. Chanté shivered.

Lane raised his hand and snapped. "Stay on mission, you two."

Chanté's eyes closed and she blushed. "Sorry. No sign of him, but he's definitely got men around."

"Who?" Monica leaned down and whispered the words, disguised as a kiss, against Chanté's cheek.

She gulped before she could answer. "Kenny's been marking them with their drinks. Everyone with a lime on the rim is someone I've seen with Stepanov before."

Kierra turned and kissed Lane's cheek as his head shifted so that he could scan the room. He settled his hand on Chanté's thigh and tapped four times to indicate the four agents.

Chanté licked her lips and nodded. "I can't say that that's all of them, but those are the ones I know I've seen before."

When Lane turned back, Kierra turned to the room. She saw a few of the agents with limes on their drinks and then spotted Kenny behind the bar, smiling and chatting with one of the dancers who was clearly flirting with him.

When Kierra turned around, Monica's one finger was gliding over Chanté's lips, over her chin and down her neck. She stopped just above the other woman's cleavage and traveled up again. Kierra was so mesmerized by that finger that it took her a second to realize that Monica was speaking, but not to them. She turned to Lane and he whispered through gritted teeth, "earpiece."

She nodded and leaned forward. She licked his lips and he spoke into her open mouth. "If you see Stepanov, take him out."

Kierra gasped.

"We're outnumbered. No need to take any chances," he breathed against her lips.

"You always take chances," Kierra said.

His eyes were intent upon hers. "Not with you."

"Jesus," Chanté whispered and began fanning herself. "Are they always this intense with you?"

Kierra could feel the smile trying to break free and she tried to keep it restrained, but it was a lost cause. She turned to Chanté, but locked eyes with Monica instead. She unconsciously ground herself against Lane's crotch. He groaned and shifted his hips against her. Monica licked her lips, her finger stilling just above Chanté's cleavage as she watched them.

And then Monica's eyes cleared, and her body stiffened. "Stepanov's car is approaching."

"Showtime," Lane breathed and then placed a soft kiss to Kierra's cheek, shifting her off him.

"Go to the back and stay there. Do not leave the building until one of us comes for you," Monica said to Chanté.

"Yes, ma'am," Chanté said and then stood. She turned to Kierra and smiled. "Would it be too weird for our new friendship if I told you that I'm going to go fuck myself crazy thinking about you three?"

"A little," Kierra said.

Chanté leaned forward and kissed Kierra's cheek quickly. "Then pretend I never said anything." With that she turned and sauntered away as if nothing urgent was happening.

Monica reached up to pull Kierra onto the couch. "It's not Stepanov," she said. "It's his boyfriend. Sergei Petrov."

"What does that mean?" She asked.

"That Stepanov is a fucking coward," Lane said just as Stepanov's boyfriend/assistant walked into the room.

It was like a flip switched. The four men that Chanté had identified immediately stood and flanked the man, the music stopped, and the lights raised slightly. Everyone who didn't know what was happening at least had the wherewithal to know that something dangerous was on the horizon. Dancers slipped off stage and horny men moved as quietly and quickly as they could to the exit.

Sergei zeroed in on their couch and began to make his way toward them. One of the guards hurried ahead and placed a chair on the other side of their small, low table. They watched as Sergei lowered himself elegantly into it.

Monica squeezed Kierra's hand before moving to graze her thigh and then rested her hand on her own knee. Kierra belatedly realized what the lust had clouded; Monica's dress was a really great cover for a whole lot of weaponry.

"Mr. and Mrs. Hudson," he said in a Russian accent. "If those are your names."

"Does it matter?" Lane responded in an irritated tone.

"I guess it does not. My employer has come to make a deal."

Kierra raised an eyebrow. A deal. A fucking deal. They'd tried to kill her at least twice and now they wanted to make a deal?

Monica clearly felt as incredulous as she did because her voice was dripping in disbelief and annoyance. "This should be interesting."

Sergei ignored her. Which made Kierra irrationally angry.

"We're listening," Lane said, his voice tight with fury.

"My employer is willing to forgive your trespass against him for an even exchange."

"Meaning?" Lane rolled his hand to indicate that Sergei should keep talking and faster.

Kierra agreed. This whole exchange was bad tv movie dramatic.

"Meaning that if you give him her," he said, finally deigning to look at Kierra, "to do with as he pleases, he will let you both live."

There was a brief moment of stunned silence before Kierra, Lane and Monica burst into near hysterical laughter.

"Is that a fucking joke?" Lane asked, wiping tears from his eyes. "Jesus, how are all of you fucking corrupt pieces of shit so entitled and dim?"

And then Kierra had another one of those moments where so many things were happening all at once that she had a problem keeping track. Lane jumped up from the couch, a gun firing in one hand while he grabbed one of their drinks from the table and smashed it into the face of the Serbian guard closest to him. His next shot went directly into the fallen man's forehead. Kierra thought he'd missed his first shot, but he'd actually been aiming at the sprinkler system. When the water started falling, the remaining guards were shocked, but only for a second before they lurched forward and fell unmoving to the ground. Kenny stood behind them, a gun in each hand.

pink slip

Kierra didn't see what happened to the last guard closest to Monica. It was only when he fell twitching to the ground that she spotted the knife sticking out of his right eye. She decided to look away.

Monica moved, pulling Sergei up from his chair, a very large knife with a curved blade on one side and a small serrated edge on the other at his throat.

Monica's dress had been pulled apart and, just as Kierra had suspected, underneath she wore a simple bandeau dress covered in a harness strapped across her chest, full of knives and brass knuckles and a lock-picking set for Lane, which Kierra irrationally thought was very sweet.

"Now we're going to counter with a deal of our own," Monica said in a terrifying whisper.

Kierra couldn't blame Sergei for shaking like a leaf in her hold. But she could blame him for pissing his pants. She looked up at him in disgust. "Your boyfriend's bff was a fucking European dictator. Have some self-respect," Kierra said.

"You tell your boss that he has two options and twenty-four hours to make a choice. Either he turns himself in to local authorities or we kill him."

"That goes double for you," Lane added.

"You're going to regret this," Sergei spat.

Lane sighed and shook his head. "I feel like you're not taking my wife's threats seriously."

Sergei spat something at them in Russian that Kierra didn't understand but it was apparently so offensive that both Lane and Kenny aimed their guns at his head. Kierra cringed as the odor of his loosened bowels filled the air between them.

"Jesus, dude," she said and pinched her nose shut.

Monica's hand moved too fast for her to see, but she assumed that Sergei's cries meant that she hadn't slit his throat. He was crouched on the ground crying, blood seeping from his head. His ear lay on the floor beneath him.

"If you move fast enough, you can relay our message to your employer and get to a hospital," Monica said, just a bit louder than her normal speaking voice to make sure that he could hear.

If Kierra hadn't been holding her nose, she might have snorted with laughter. That would have been inappropriate and mean, so she pressed her lips together. She watched as Sergei pressed one hand to the right side of his head, grasped his ear from the ground and ran awkwardly in his soiled pants to the exit.

"He's coming your way," Lane said. Kierra assumed he was speaking to Asif.

"Pssst," a voice said from behind them.

When Kierra turned, she almost wanted to laugh at Chanté's head poking through the curtains. "Can I come out now?"

"Are you kidding me? We told you to hide until we came to get you." Lane yelled.

"I know, but I'm nosy," she said.

Lane let out an exaggerated sigh as Chanté walked toward them. Kierra noted that she'd changed into a pair of black jeans and a loose deep V-neck t-shirt and she was sad about it.

"Alright, you take them back to the safe house," Lane said to Kenny. "We'll handle Stepanov."

"You said he had twenty-four hours?" Kierra asked.

"We lied," Monica replied simply. She moved to belt her dress and Kierra stood.

The thought descended on her that this scene was like Serbia and her heart began to beat faster, much faster than it had when there was a literal gun and knife fight happening in front of her. She didn't want to interrogate that too much in the moment, it wasn't as important as walking into Monica's arms.

She could feel the harness between them, but she pressed closer still. "I'm going with you."

"Oh girl, no," Chanté mumbled in soft judgment.

"It's too dangerous," Monica said.

"Is this a made-for-tv spy movie now?" Kenny asked in disgust.

Kierra ignored them both.

"And then what?" It was supremely bad timing but that seemed very on brand for this entire messy affair. And Kierra refused to let them walk away from her in this club the way they had in Serbia.

"You said in Serbia that this was the end of the road. But I'm not done with you two," she said, tears springing to her eyes. "I let you send me away once, but if you do it again, this is it. It's really over and I don't ever want to see either of you again."

Lane moved to press himself against Kierra's back. "Kenny's just going to take you back to the safe house. We'll kill Stepanov and be right back," he said and pressed a kiss to the back of her head.

"Oh," Kierra said, her face warming in embarrassment. Could it really be that easy? "Well see you in a bit, I guess."

Monica smiled and gripped Kierra's chin between her thumb and finger. "You're very fucking adorable, sweet girl."

"And sexy," Kierra prompted.

"Very sexy," Lane chuckled into her hair.

They pulled away from her and walked briskly toward the front exit.

Kenny moved in the other direction and raised his gun. "Follow me."

Chanté reached out for Kierra's hand and she grasped it, taking one last look over her shoulder. She sent a silent prayer after Monica and Lane, hoping they would be okay.

"You three are so sweet," Chanté whispered. "And fucking hot."

Kierra couldn't help the laugh that bubbled up from her chest.

"Shh," Kenny hissed.

Oh right. The mission.

Monica

Monica had always believed that she was a good person at her core. But there was something about the calm that overtook her when she had a gun in one hand and the other resting on the hilt of a knife that made her question whether that wasn't a delusion. How could she be a good person and a good agent at the same time? After a few years in The Agency she'd given up the moral quandary as a moot point. She was good at her job and she enjoyed the work, there wasn't any reason to complicate her life any further. But then Kierra had waltzed into an abandoned airport hangar like a lamb on its way to slaughter, all doe-eyed innocence, and upended the life Monica and Lane had built, bringing those old questions to the surface again.

Suddenly it mattered that the trafficker she'd sniped had a family. And it mattered that she slept like a baby after a kill. It was of the utmost importance that she could remember the face of every kill she'd made, but not necessarily all their names. These small idiosyncrasies grew around a larger point of contention. Because suddenly any deep cover job that required that she and Lane be away from home for more than a night or two held less and less appeal. The separation from Kierra didn't seem worth it. And that was before Serbia.

For three years she'd told herself that they could just want Kierra without ever having her. They could enjoy the shameless flirtation of her skimpy outfits and infatuation and hide their own longing. It never had to be more than that, because no matter how she twisted and turned the dilemma over in her head, she had finally come to the truth of it: she and Lane were not good people. And any more intimate encounters with them would only put Kierra in danger.

But then Serbia happened and all those boundaries that Monica had used to protect Kierra from them and their own hearts from her for three years went up in smoke. And then Serbia had ended, and Monica had had to accept that they couldn't go back. They never stood a chance.

She'd spent three months listing, feeling as if there was a puzzle piece missing from the grand scheme of their world, but unwilling to admit it. Seeing Kierra for the first time in too long had felt eerily like seeing Lane for the first time on campus that day all those years ago; as if a piece of herself she hadn't known was missing had been slotted into place. Now they had her back, almost, and Monica wasn't going to let anything get in the way of that.

Asif gestured with his hands that there were two guards down the hall on either side. He nodded once before launching himself into the hallway, his gun raised high. He shot the guard on his left while Lane, crouched at Monica's feet, aimed and shot the other.

They'd tracked Sergei across town to a luxurious hotel in the city's financial district. The tracker Monica has surreptitiously placed on his body indicated that he was in the penthouse. It had taken half an hour for Asif to hack into the security system, but once he had they'd been able to ride the service elevator up to the top floor undetected. He wouldn't compromise their communication silence, but Monica knew that Lane was going to launch into a very long speech about European dictators with the worst security systems once this mission was over. She'd sat through some version of it before and was not looking forward to having to half-hear it again. But she reminded herself, Kierra was back at the safe house. Monica would happily listen to Lane drone on and on about firewalls and double-blind passwords and whatever the fuck else was missing from a shocking number of criminals' homes, if she could do so with Kierra, and eventually Lane, in her arms.

Monica brought up the rear, walking backward down the hallway, a gun in each hand aimed in the general radius of center mass should anyone suddenly appear and interrupt them. Asif used the keycard he'd fished from a guard's pocket and dipped it into the card reader. It beeped and unlocked. He slowly pulled the handle up and pushed the door just barely open. They held position, waiting for any unusual sounds from the room that might indicate a trap or some other sticky situation that Lane and Asif would be happy to shoot their way through. When they were satisfied that the coast was as clear as it was ever going to be, Asif slowly pushed the door fully open. He stayed low while Monica and Lane took cover on either side of the door jamb. They moved into the penthouse foyer slowly, crouching low, guns cocked.

The room was silent. Or at least they thought it was silent until they heard the heavy panting and grunting coming from the room across the sitting area that Monica assumed was the bedroom. She turned to look at Lane who was shaking his head in disbelief. They had killed all of Sergei's guards, cut off his boyfriend's ear and threatened his life and Stepanov was horny.

Granted, Monica could relate. Their lives were on the line but there had been a moment back at Menagerie when Kierra had straddled Lane and looked at her, a challenge in her normally submissive gaze. Monica had seriously considered shooting a few slugs into the ceiling and kicking everyone out of the building. Except for Chanté, who wasn't really Monica's type but when she'd seen the way Kierra's eyes had glued onto Chanté's thick thighs, she'd decided then and there that Chanté could be her type for tonight. Anything for Kierra.

They moved swiftly, but cautiously, across the sitting area. Lane crouched to pull the door handle down, but Monica shot her hand out and gripped his shoulder. She tilted her head to indicate that she wanted to take the lead on this. He shook his head no. His eyes were wide with shock and fear. An unusual mix for him.

Lane never disobeyed her orders. Monica knew he suspected that she was compromised. And she was willing to accept that he was probably right. But he also knew that she was the best shot of the three of them. And Stepanov had threatened Kierra's life. So, she was also very dangerous.

She raised her eyebrows in a silent challenge that Lane wanted to meet but couldn't. Their missions only worked if there was clear leadership. And that leadership was Monica. It always had been, and it always would be. They both knew that Lane would follow her wherever she led, even if it was straight into the line of fire. But this time, she just wanted to handle business and lead him home. To Kierra. Finally.

After a tense moment, where Monica could see that he was waging an internal battle, he finally nodded at her, a tight dip of his head. He shifted out of her way, pulled the door handle down and pushed it open.

Monica hung back as the people inside yelled and scrambled.

A volley of shots sprayed through the door. Lane had moved out of the doorway just in time. They stood there waiting as a voice they recognized as Stepanov's yelled in Serbian for his guards. Another voice they recognized as Sergei's prayed. And then one more voice that Monica didn't recognize simply wailed.

But they waited. Asif and Lane looked at Monica, their eyes beseeching her to give the word for them to move in and finish this. But Monica was not brash. She didn't have Lane's outgoing charm or the recklessness of most of her male colleagues. She was smart and patient and the best fucking spy in The Agency for a reason. She waited and waited and waited until she heard Stepanov clamoring off the bed and rushing toward the bedroom door, cursing for his guards. He assumed that one of them had been secretly watching them have sex. Not that that his reckoning was coming.

It was a gamble, one that Lane might have taken, but not a foolish one. Monica couldn't peek around the door into the room or else she would give her position away. So she had to turn into the doorway blind, gun already raised, search for her target and fire in the second or so before Stepanov realized what was happening. Stepanov's steps faltered as she came into view, his frustration shifting to fear as recognition contorted his face. She shot him dead center in the forehead before he could even get his index finger back on the trigger.

The aftermath was all sound and confusion.

Sergei threw his body onto Stepanov, crying in anguish, a crude bandage wrapped over his missing ear. Monica could only look down on him in judgement; crying for a man who wouldn't send him to a hospital to get his ear reattached because he was horny was not an emotion that she could relate to. The other man in the room seemed to deflate; Monica couldn't tell if it was from exhaustion or relief.

Lane called for their local cleanup crew – which was really a small cell of Agency operatives embedded in the police department – to take Sergei and the other man into custody. When they arrived, Monica's team slipped out of the room. The pushed into the stairwell, walked down two flights and rode the main elevator to the lobby. As the doors opened, Monica draped her body around Asif's frame, seeming to whisper into his ear, while Lane started to tell a completely fictional story about a Hooters bar in El Paso and a wing eating contest as loud as he could in his thick Texas accent.

Monica feigned a slight stumble as they walked through the lobby, giving the illusion of intoxication. They walked at a leisurely pace out the front door, turned left and then, at the corner, right heading toward the crowded main drag of this posh tourist section of downtown Berlin.

Once they were far enough away, Monica straightened and pushed away from Asif, who turned toward them, a wicked smile on his face.

"Well, this was real," he said saluting at them.

"You're not coming back to the safe house?" Normally she wouldn't have asked the question. In fact, normally splitting up would be the smartest move they could make. But Chanté.

Monica watched that exact train of thought flicker over Asif's features. His will seemed to falter, but then he shook his head, his smile widened, and he began to back away from them.

"Make sure she gets her regular pay and my bonus," was all he said before he jogged across the street and jumped into a cab idling at the corner.

Monica watched him, stuck somewhere between disbelief that he could abandon his asset, and the woman he clearly loved – even if that love was complicated – and total understanding. Because she and Lane had done exactly that once. They'd strolled away from Kierra, walking through Club Ménage as if she wasn't behind them, her heart breaking, their hearts breaking, just three months before.

She turned to Lane. "Let's go," she said, tilting her head in the opposite direction.

"But-" Lane started. Monica shook her head.

"That's none of our business," she said, grasping his left hand in her right, their fingers tangling naturally. She didn't have to say anything else, because it was clear. Asif and Chanté's mess wasn't any of their business because they had to get back to Kierra.

Lane turned his head to watch the cab's taillights disappear in the distance. Monica kept her gaze forward, leading Lane home.

seventeen

Kierra couldn't believe how normal it all seemed. They'd driven back to the safe house as if they'd just spent a regular night out. Chanté and Kenny fought over which terrible Europop station to listen to as if Monica hadn't cut a man's ear off. Kierra sat in the back seat, watching to make sure no one was following them, but also singing along to a Robyn song she'd loved in college.

She and Chanté had clung to one another standing in the foyer, while Kenny had gone through the house and checked to make sure that it hadn't been compromised.

"I really like your perfume," Kierra whispered to Chanté.

"Thanks. Asif bought it for me."

Kierra squinted at her in the dim room. "Asif doesn't seem like the perfume buying type."

"Sorry, I meant I hacked his credit card and bought this for myself." She smiled sweetly at Kierra.

"He's like a spy. Should his credit card be hackable?"

"Sweetheart, everything is hackable. If it's not nailed down or a figment of someone's imagination, it's asking to be stolen."

Kierra chuckled. "When they said you were a thief, I thought they meant a pickpocket. But you're like a hacker. Like a real-life hacker?"

Chanté tried to pretend that she wasn't ecstatic to hear that her reputation preceded her. But she ruined her valiant effort by curtseying, which made Kierra laugh louder than she'd meant to.

"I am," Chanté said. "But I can also pick your pocket. Only… that dress barely has enough fabric to cover your ass, let alone hide any valuables." She raked an appreciative lustful glare over Kierra's body. "Besides, I mostly try to keep my thieving to corrupt corporate executives and Asif."

"You two have a very strange relationship," Kierra whispered.

"You're dating a married couple. Define strange."

Kierra nodded, "Okay, fair point. But we're not dating. Not technically."

"So what are you doing?"

Kierra opened her mouth to answer, completely unsure of what words would come out of her mouth because she honestly didn't know, when Kenny turned on the living room lights and came back to the foyer. "All clear," he said. "Who's hungry?"

"Me," Chanté yelled, jumping up and down. "I can make toast if anyone's interested."

"No toast," Kenny called over his shoulder, heading to the kitchen. "I need real food."

And that was how Monica and Lane found them, standing around the kitchen island, eating sandwiches and listening to Chanté's impassioned treatise about why a pair of six-inch acrylic heels were actually the perfect weapon. They'd been so engrossed in her story that they didn't even hear Monica and Lane enter the safe house until they were practically in the kitchen.

Kenny stood up straight. "How'd it go?"

Monica nodded at him but looked at Kierra to answer. "Stepanov's dead. It's over."

"Are you sure? Is Sergei going to come after me next?"

"I doubt it. He knows what will happen if he does."

Kierra sighed in relief, slumping against the kitchen island. How odd that it had all ended while she was eating half a turkey club. She'd expected something a little more dramatic on her end.

"Where's Asif?" Chanté's voice was a tangle of emotions that Kierra did not want to experience; fear and disbelief and hurt and anger.

Monica answered in a calm, quiet voice that Kierra found she liked the way she liked every version of Monica's voice:

reverently. "He's fine. We split up. He said to give you his bonus. And Kenny will take you wherever you want to go."

Chanté's smile faltered for a brief second before rebounding in full force. But her happiness didn't meet her eyes anymore. "Okay," she said. And maybe if everyone else's eyes were closed they might have believed her. She turned to Kenny and smiled, "Want to run away to Amsterdam with me?"

He rolled his eyes at her but swiveled his head to Monica, silently asking for permission.

"It's best that we all get away from here as quickly as possible. Amsterdam is just as good as any other city. Someone will be in touch about your next assignment when the time is right."

He nodded, turned to Lane and nodded again. And then he turned to Kierra and smiled. "So do you still hate me?"

She had to laugh at that. Their first meeting at the Dublin airport felt like years ago. But it had only been a week. It was hard to believe that this smiling man with the strong jaw and broad chest was the same person who'd coaxed a days-long migraine from her as the annoying social director of a fake writer's retreat. She shook her head, "Not as much."

He laughed and turned to Chanté. "Come on then. Let's go get arrested."

She turned to Kierra and stage whispered. "He's just joking. He hates jail." Chanté pulled her into a tight squeeze. "I'm really happy Stepanov didn't kill you."

Kierra didn't know exactly what to say to that, so she squeezed Chanté harder and hoped that conveyed everything she was feeling, which ranged from strong glee that she wasn't dead to a sad sorrow that Asif wasn't a better man.

Chanté and Kenny slipped out of the kitchen. Kierra wondered if she'd ever see them again.

When it was just the three of them alone in the silent kitchen, Monica and Lane standing at one end of the island, Kierra at the other, she could feel all the day's stresses beginning to catch up with her. She opened her mouth to speak but Lane cut her off.

"Hold that thought. We need to get out of here as quickly as possible."

"You said it's over," Kierra said.

"It is, but the best jobs are get in and get out. You never want to be around just in case someone decides they want some revenge," Monica said.

"Okay. So where are we going?"

The right side of Monica's mouth tipped up into a sly grin. "Wherever you want, sweet girl," she said.

Kierra recognized the utter absurdity of her life. She truly did. In the past few months she'd seen more guns and knives being used to maim or kill more people than she would have imagined as a very normal aspiring poet. But she'd also rarely felt safer than when she was with the two people standing in front of her.

"Paris," Kierra said, smiling brightly. "I've always wanted to go to Paris."

"Then let's get the hell out of here," Lane laughed.

"On one condition," Kierra said.

"Another damn condition?" Lane breathed, bringing his hands on his hips.

"Last one," she said, holding out her hands.

"Anything," Monica said, all serious and deadly just like Kierra liked her.

"I want my old job back," she breathed warily.

Kierra held her breath in anticipation until Lane burst out laughing, the sound of it washing over her like joy. "That's it?"

"What do you mean, 'that's it?'"

He turned to Monica and gestured toward Kierra. "Can you tell her now?"

Kierra turned to Monica who seemed to be fighting a smile. "We might have forgotten to process your resignation. Just in case."

"Just in case what?" Kierra shrieked.

"Just in case you ever wanted to come back to us," Lane said, matter-of-factly, as if he was making sense.

"But I- In Serbia, I said I didn't want to leave." She threw her hands up into the air. She didn't know if Chanté and Kenny were still around to hear this and she didn't care.

Lane watched her with amusement in his eyes. "How would you know if you really wanted to be here if you never left?"

He asked the question so simply that she wanted to punch him. It was a good question. Clear and to the point. And he was right. If they'd asked her to sign a ten-year contract in that tiny hallway in Club Ménage, she would have done it without even thinking. She'd been so hopped up on the adrenaline and lust of the experience, especially the part having to do with sex, that she'd have blindly followed them to the ends of the earth. But she'd never have known if that was truly the right decision for her.

"We owed you that at least," Monica said.

Kierra rolled her eyes and walked past them out of the kitchen. "Well, you still could have sent me a postcard or something while I was unemployed."

"We'll remember that next time," Lane said.

"What next time? It's going to take an act of Congress for you two to get rid of me." She turned to smile at them over her shoulder. They followed her up to their room and watched as she threw the few toiletries she'd used back into her suitcase and zipped it up.

"And just so we're clear," she said as they threw their bags into the car. "You're still not allowed to touch me until I say so."

"Yes, boss," Lane said and pulled away from the safe house. The night was still dark. By the time morning came they'd all be in different countries, using different aliases. But she, Lane and Monica would be together at least. And that was more than she'd let herself hope for in years.

***

They were supposed to go out and be extra touristy. Monica and Lane had been to Paris more times than they could remember, but only ever on missions. This unexpected vacation was a chance for them to see the city for the first time as normal people. They were just a regular Canadian couple – per their new set of IDs – enjoying a holiday with their American girlfriend. But it had been raining all day. They decided to skip the tourist attractions and were holed up in their hotel suite, pretending to consider a vast array of options for their indoor amusement over room service breakfast.

Kierra was on the phone with Maya, reassuring her that she was fine and had just decided to travel around Europe for a little while after the writer's retreat. "The retreat was great," she lied.

Monica turned to Lane with an arched eyebrow.

"Yea, I wrote so much, caught up on my sleep." She paused and listened, her forehead wrinkling in confusion. "Okay well, it's a turn of phrase. I slept a lot. Better?"

Monica stood from her chair. Lane's eyes drank her in as if he were a starving, dehydrated man. And in many ways, he was. She stopped behind Kierra's chair and massaged her shoulders. Kierra tilted her head back to look up at her. Technically, they still weren't allowed to touch her yet, but he could see the end of that prohibition on the horizon.

Now that she had Kierra's attention, Monica raised a hand and slowly beckoned Lane to her with one crooked finger. She smiled at Kierra and then walked toward their bedroom.

"Hey Maya, I have to go. I think my cell company charges like a dollar a minute for these calls."

Monica turned around in the room and Lane pulled her to him, crushing his mouth to hers. Kierra rushed into the room after them. They turned to look at her and he wanted to laugh at her wide eyes, as if she'd never seen them kiss before. She was panting already.

"Since we can't touch you yet-" Monica paused to see if Kierra would correct her. She didn't, so she continued, "It looks like I'm going to have to fuck him instead." Kierra nodded, but he was sure that she didn't understand. The coming surprise thrilled him.

He stepped back and untied the silky robe covering her naked body. His hands skimmed the tops of her breasts and her strong shoulders before pushing the fabric from her. Letting it drift delicately to the floor.

"There's something in that bag behind you. Can you bring it to me?"

Lane licked his thumbs and circled Monica's nipples gently until they hardened. He lowered his head to suck one into his mouth, smiling around the soft flesh.

Kierra gasped. Now she understood.

"Really?"

"Don't forget the lube," Monica gasped and cupped his head.

Kierra rushed back to them, Monica's harness and dildo and the lube clutched tight to her chest. "I take it back. You can touch me. You can do anything you want to me."

Lane stood up straight and grasped Monica behind the neck. "After," he said, pulling her into another kiss.

***

She was gentle with Lane. Gentler than he normally liked. But this time wasn't just for the two of them. Monica penetrated his ass slowly, enjoying the way he gasped and groaned for more, and the way Kierra's hands smoothed along his back, soothing him, her eyes locked on Monica's dildo slowly sinking into his body.

"Does it hurt?" She whispered the question and Monica was unsure if she meant it to be heard and expected an answer.

"The good kind of hurt," Lane said. He groaned.

178

Monica was finally fully inside him. She locked eyes with Kierra, their hands meeting as they both rubbed his back in soothing sweeps.

"But if you're worried about me, you could get on your back and let me taste you."

Monica smiled. Leave it to Lane to be full of Monica, his hips trying to writhe on her dick, but still managing to seduce Kierra. She couldn't blame her for smiling shyly as she laid back, welcoming Lane's head between her thighs.

Kierra's hips jerked when Lane's mouth settled over her pussy. Monica saw it as a sign that it was time for her to move. Kierra grasped her breasts, one in each hand and rolled her nipples. Her eyes drifted closed and then sprung open again. She didn't want to miss a thing. Monica smiled at that and ground her hips into Lane harder.

He lifted his head to groan loudly. Kierra moved one of her hands to the back of his head, directing him back to her sex. She was always great at keeping him on task.

Monica kept her pace slow so that she could drink in the scene in front of her and keep Lane balanced on the edge of wanting; teasing him to draw out his pleasure the way he was stringing Kierra's desire along. She couldn't see but she knew how he liked to work, light touches of his tongue interspersed with hard suction and a finger or two before he retreated again, his panting breaths on her wet sex ramping up his partner's arousal. She'd come undone more times than she could remember under the ministrations of his skillful mouth.

When Kierra came, her back arched, she pinched her nipples hard between her fingers as she chanted "oh fuck oh fuck oh fuck". Monica was so enraptured by the sights and sounds of it that she only just caught the movement of Lane's hand, probably wet from Kierra's orgasm underneath his body, surely grasping his dick.

"Fuck let me come," he moaned. "Please."

Monica kept her eyes on Kierra's breasts; they bounced minutely as she panted. Monica started to fuck Lane in earnest. He had wrapped his arm around Kierra's legs, his face flat against her stomach, holding her close as he came apart. Monica's fingers dug into Lane's hips and she fucked him in sure, long strokes just like he liked it until he was a sweaty mess between her and Kierra, begging for her to stop. This was how she wanted every day to be.

***

Kierra was lying in their hotel's king-sized bed wondering a few things.

First, she was wondering if she should create a pen name for the erotic poetry that she had just now, while watching Monica fuck Lane into a stupor, decided to write. She'd hate to think that her aunt would be at the local bookstore or browsing online, see her name, buy her book and then settle into bed with a hot cup of tea and suddenly find herself reading the sonnet she planned to write about Monica's breasts, or the haiku about the way Lane tasted on her tongue.

That felt wrong.

Second, she was thinking about what it might feel like to have Lane and Monica inside her at the same time.

But it was the third thought that she said aloud. "So, am I eligible for a raise?"

Lane laughed weakly and Monica smiled as she took off her strap-on and settled onto the bed next to her. She trailed her finger up Kierra's naked torso, just barely touching her. That whispered touch felt like electricity. Kierra arched her back trying to get closer, to have more, but Monica moved her hand away.

"You have to submit the request in writing," Monica said.

Lane crawled up the bed and collapsed on his back next to Monica. "We'd have to send the request and our recommendation to HR."

"Wait, The Agency has an HR department?"

"Of course it does," Monica said. She dragged her index finger around and around Kierra's left nipple and then moved to do the same with the right.

"Well how was I supposed to know? I mean, I have been dressing and acting very unprofessionally for three years. I just assumed that since I never heard from HR that it didn't exist."

"That's actually a fair assumption. And technically we're going to get written up once we tell them what we've been doing with you all over Europe," Lane breathed.

"And what we plan to do to you once we get back home," Monica added.

Kierra shivered at her words, and also because that same index finger was tracing its way down her rib cage, circling her stomach and drifting through the soft curly hair atop her mound.

"If you get the raise-"

"Which you probably will," Monica interjected.

"It'll come contingent on applying for higher clearance and increased responsibilities."

Kierra moaned and opened her legs as Monica dragged that one finger up and down her sex. "Like what responsibilities?"

"Nothing big," Monica said, swiping her tongue across Kierra's nipple. "Unless you want to be trained to handle more sensitive intel. If you did that, you'd be tier two administrative support. You'd see a very significant pay raise once that was complete."

"Am I tier one now?"

"Technically no," Lane said, turning to his side to watch Monica play with Kierra's body.

Kierra blew out a breath and then her hips jerked as Monica slipped two fingers inside of her.

"If you take the course, you wouldn't be just our PA anymore. You'd become vital support staff," Monica said.

"Normally they recruit for that. They like graduates with strong computer skills and law enforcement training."

"I'm just a poet. Oh fuck," Kierra said, her sex clenching around Monica's fingers as the orgasm washed over her.

"After Serbia we had to debrief. You handled yourself really well for someone with no espionage training. You're not the usual recruit, but you're more than capable," Monica said.

Kierra was floating, hearing what Monica was saying but not quite processing. Monica's head listed forward, and she pressed her forehead to Kierra's shoulder. She turned to see Lane wrapped around Monica from the back, their bodies slowly rocking together. She shifted, turning to her side and reached a hand down between Monica's legs. She circled Monica's clit with her fingers and placed soft kisses on her face. Lane began to fuck her faster and harder.

When Monica was close, another question came to Kierra. "How big is the raise exactly?"

"Yes yes yes," Monica yelled, pulling Kierra's body closer to hers.

Kierra wasn't sure if those yeses were some sort of answer to her question, but she leaned forward and kissed Lane while Monica trembled between them. She'd find out eventually. There was absolutely no need to rush.

epilogue

The safe house in London never struck Kenny as particularly fortified at first glance. From the street it looked like an old brick squat house, slim and deep and vertical like all the other houses surrounding it. It was set in the middle of what used to be a working-class neighborhood in East London. Now the community was a mix of displaced workers from all over the city just barely holding onto city dwelling before being pushed out of the capitol once and for all. Littered amongst them were wealthy hipsters mostly living off their parents' wealth while trying to stay forever on the wave of the newest, trendiest places to live. And then there were The Agency's two safe houses.

Kenny nodded minutely at Mrs. Wilde who was pretending to water the fake plants in her front garden as the sun set behind them. He lifted the keypad on the door, pressed his thumb against the sensor and waited for it to beep. When it did, he input his personal pin and the front door unlocked.

Inside, the air smelled faintly of cloves, which meant he'd just missed Asif. "Coward," he muttered under his breath.

He did a quick scan of the bottom floors of the house, opening every door, checking every window, making sure it was secure. As Monica said, "No safe house can protect you from your own stupidity." He'd had to wait six hours to jot that down in the notebook he kept of whatever brilliant pieces of knowledge she offhandedly offered him because they'd been on a stakeout. But it was seared in his head, like almost everything she said or did.

Asif would have called it a crush and he would have been wrong. It was professional adoration, pure and simple. Kenny didn't want to sleep with Monica – not least because Lane and

Kierra would probably maim him if he tried – he wanted to be her.

Besides, she wasn't his type.

He took the small, shallow stairs to the attic room. He closed and locked the door behind him and tried to pretend that it was only the exhaustion that had his heart beating fast against his chest. He pulled his fitted gray t-shirt over his head and checked his watch. He had half an hour before his appointment. He pulled off the rest of his clothes on the way to the bathroom.

The shower was scalding hot and fast. He swiped at the foggy mirror while he brushed his teeth. He turned his head left to right and considered if he had enough time to shave, which was foolish, but he considered it anyway. In the end he decided that there wasn't enough time. He sprayed himself with cologne, which also felt stupid, but again, he did it anyway. Tonight was special. These appointments were always special.

Kenny moved across the room, naked, and rummaged through his luggage.

"The key to being a good spy is to be comfortable traveling light." That was another thing Monica had once said and Kenny had imbibed the message as if it were gospel. He'd heard it first when she gave a talk to his recruitment class five years ago. He'd been cocky, green and searching desperately for a mentor. And then there she was, standing in front of him looking deadly and bored. She hadn't known it, but Kenny had decided right in that moment that she was the kind of agent he wanted to be, and he'd unofficially adopted her as mentor, life coach, role model.

Granted, the last three months had revealed that just because it sounded good, didn't mean that it was truly reflective of real life. Because what had their most recent mission been if not the definition of too much baggage? But Kenny wasn't the same person today that he'd been five years ago. He liked to think that he was wiser and more experienced. He was certainly more built. He was also dumb as a sack of rocks. Because five years ago Kenny would never have let himself get into this mess.

He fished his laptop and a bottle of lube from his bag and settled in the middle of the bed.

It had been a long two weeks. After leaving Berlin, he and Chanté had meandered to Amsterdam. But it had been less like a buddy road trip and more like babysitting – as he'd tried to stop her from grifting and thieving just because she could – and therapy, since she'd spent every night dancing away her heartbreak before crying herself to sleep around four in the morning. When they'd finally split up, Chanté had seemed hollowed out and depressed. He'd put her on a plane back to her family in Detroit, hoping that the time away would rejuvenate her.

His hatred of Asif had grown exponentially.

He'd just entered the UK when he'd received a message that it was time to get back to D.C. and attend to his other missions. There was actually a lot he needed to do. He was running some passive surveillance ops on the arms and drug trade out of Serbia, Chechnya and Albania that were pressing. And he still needed to file a mission report from Berlin, although every time he'd tried to work on it, it either turned into an erotic romance-thriller or a half-page list of Agency resources used with no narrative. He couldn't figure out how to lie, without lying, or if he even needed to lie. But all of that could wait until later.

He logged into his personal account on the laptop and navigated his browser quickly to the ChatBot website. He signed in quickly and was at her personal page in a heartbeat. His presence was announced in the public group chat room.

MasquerAsiaN has logged in.

He tried not to let himself get too gassed up, but he couldn't help but hope that the way Maya's eyes lit up was for him. There was a bit of a delay in the chat room feed, but he thought it was a possibility. And then he thought he was fucking pathetic.

ThickaThanASnicka
Hey stranger, @MasquerAsiaN

He smiled and typed,

MasquerAsiaN
It's Thursday

ThickaThanASnicka
So it is ;)

He sent the private chat request and waited as she said goodbye to the chatroom, blowing a kiss to her webcam.

He asked for an hour, even though he wanted two. Her current rates were $100/hour for dirty chat and manual masturbation and rose as the degree of difficulty, as she liked to call it, increased. He'd spent a lot of time thinking about what he wanted. He always did. He couldn't help but use the seven days between their regular appointments to fantasize about every kinky thing he wanted to watch her do to herself at his instruction and everything he longed to do to her in person.

He chose manual masturbation because he'd been having a craving, but he increased her rate to $250, which was still far less than she deserved.

She accepted his invitation and payment immediately.

While he waited for their private chat to load, he reached behind him to grasp the lube. He put a small drop in the center of his left palm and began to rub it slowly up and down his shaft, warming himself up for her.

When her face popped on the screen, he felt his heart constrict and his index finger unconsciously hovered over the button that would turn on his laptop's internal web camera. He didn't press it, but he desperately wanted to.

"Hi stranger," she said again. Hearing the words come out of her mouth always felt like a gift that he didn't deserve.

MasquerAsiaN
Hey beautiful

She pouted. "So you're not going to let me see you tonight?" She asked the question every week.

MasquerAsiaN
I wish I could. But my job...

He didn't finish the sentence because he couldn't bear to lie to her any more than he already had. Even though his job was technically the reason she couldn't hear or see him, it wasn't for the reasons he was leading her to believe. The ellipses made him sound like a creeping married politician or government worker (he was). He knew that human nature would let her fill in the rest of his story from there.

What mattered is that he knew she would never guess that he'd run surveillance on her roommate – and by extension her – for months. She'd never even consider that he'd just spent a week with Kierra trying to keep a corrupt Eastern European politician from killing her. Those possibilities would never enter her mind because they were so far out of the realm of her experience. Which meant that for one hour every week, he allowed himself the selfish permission not to think about how truly messed up this all was.

MasquerAsiaN
I like your lingerie.

pink slip

She smiled and bit her bottom lip. He grasped the head of his dick and exhaled through his nose. It didn't take much to get him going where she was concerned.

"This old thing?" She stuck her thumb under one strap and moved it over her shoulder playfully, briefly causing the scoop neck of the nightie to dip low and almost show him one nipple. "You said you liked me in red, so I wore it just for you."

MasquerAsiaN
I feel like the luckiest man. Please take it off.

She giggled and rearranged herself on her knees in front of her camera. She locked eyes with the lens and then slowly lifted the hem up her thighs, over her stomach, and then over her chest. She threw it to the side and stared at the camera. At him. Waiting.

He let his eyes roam over Maya's smooth light brown skin. She wasn't wearing a bra and her breasts were large, more than a handful. Much more. He licked his lips as his gaze settled on the dark tips of her breasts and her small nipples that he knew, when she got going, would grow hard and erect, begging for the attentions of his fingers or mouth or tongue. But he was thousands of miles away, in another country, hiding behind the anonymity of the internet. He didn't deserve to touch her anyway. So he typed the next best thing.

MasquerAsiaN
Play with your nipples baby.

She sat back on her heels, flashing a small sliver of the bright red panties stretched over her sex in between her large, soft thighs. Thighs that he'd dreamt about touching, licking, kissing and biting more times than he could count.

"Do you like what you see?" She asked the question in a small voice, almost as if she was nervous, unsure of the answer. But Kenny couldn't believe that was what she was thinking. Not when she looked like that and did what she did to him.

Before he typed, he poured more lube into his other hand.

MasquerAsiaN
Like isn't a strong enough word.

She was pinching her nipples.

MasquerAsiaN
Harder

She giggled and the sound was like a bolt of lightning straight from his gut to the tip of his dick.

MasquerAsiaN
You have no idea what your laugh does to me.

In the past couple of months, Kenny had become particularly adept at typing with one hand while the other was occupied. A unique skill that might serve him well as a spy one day but served him very well every Thursday. He stroked himself slowly as she rolled her nipples between her fingers. He groaned when she moved her left hand under one breast and raised it, bringing her nipple to her mouth. She swiped her tongue across the hard point, eyes on the webcam, digitally boring into his soul.

He gripped his dick hard at the base, needing to slow down.

MasquerAsiaN
Do that again.

pink slip

She clucked her tongue and smiled, "Ask nicely."

MasquerAsiaN
Please do that again.

His fingers stilled over the keys. He'd almost typed her name. Her real name. Not her screen name. It wasn't the first time he'd been on the verge of making that particular cataclysmic mistake. In an hour or two he'd think about this moment and he'd berate himself for even logging into ChatBot when he knew that he was breaking all kinds of protocols and lying to her to boot. But right now, he simply breathed and reminded himself to calm down. There was so much time left.

She was sucking insistently on her nipple, staring at the webcam. Waiting for his next direction.

MasquerAsiaN
Don't forget your other breast.
I wouldn't.

"You wouldn't?" She asked the question and then licked her beautiful mound, scraping her teeth along the nipple.

MasquerAsiaN
Jesus. One more time please.

She laughed. A full, deep-throated, throw her head back in glee laugh that he loved twice as much as the giggle. And then she gave him one more image of her perfect white teeth gliding over her dark brown nipple.

He began to move his hand faster up and down his shaft. He couldn't stop himself.

MasquerAsiaN

I wouldn't. I'd make sure that every part of you got equal attention.
All night long.

Her hips were moving in small circles now. "Mmmm, I bet you would."
MasquerAsiaN
I want to see you touch yourself.

He typed, pressed send and then added,
MasquerAsiaN
Please.

She smiled, "Good boy."

MasquerAsiaN
Don't push it. ;)

She moved her hands to her underwear and leaned forward, her breasts swaying gently, "Will you spank me if I keep on?"
He closed his eyes only briefly, letting himself imagine what it would feel like to finally get his hands on her. To glide his palms over every inch of her skin. To grasp the soft expanse of her flesh like he'd always wanted to. He could almost hear the way his palm would sound smacking her ass, the way that ripple of contact would make her body jiggle, mesmerizing him, pulling him even deeper under her spell. He had to grip the head of his dick and take a deep breath to stop himself from coming. It was too soon. But he knew he wouldn't last much longer.

MasquerAsiaN
You're killing me.

She laughed again as she moved to her back, lifting her legs in the air and shimmying her panties up her thighs and off.

MasquerAsiaN
Stay like that.
So fucking perfect.

It was the worst position. He wouldn't be able to see her play with herself, watch her fingers glide up and down her sex and slip into her pussy. But he would be able to see each gasp as she fucked herself slowly into a stupor, only speeding up when he typed that he was close, which was far better in his opinion. And that's exactly what she did.

They came together, the beautiful mounds of her body a literal feast for his eyes while her gasps and moans pulled him toward his own release. He turned up the volume on his laptop, not wanting to miss a single sound. But what broke him – and sent him right over the edge – was that small giggle that he loved when she came. It was his actual favorite thing about her. She came with her whole entire being and that laugh was the purest expression of her joy.

Kenny had never been with anyone like Maya. After two months of trying to convince himself to stop this, to turn back, because he was jeopardizing everything he'd been working for his entire life, he just couldn't stay away. Because there was no one else like Maya.

She turned to the camera, resting her head on her hand, grinning at him. "Was that as good for you as it was for me?"

MasquerAsiaN
LMAO
I just made the biggest mess.

She snorted when she laughed this time, which only made her laugh even harder.

He bolted to the bathroom, reluctantly tearing his eyes away from her face. He grabbed a towel and brought it back to the bed, cleaning himself up as he walked.

"So what do you think, babe? You got another round in you? You've still got over half an hour left."

He settled back on the bed.

MasquerAsiaN
That sounds like a challenge.

She raised one eyebrow. "It might be."
He laughed this time. Not that she could hear him.

MasquerAsiaN
Can we talk for a little bit first?

"We can do whatever you want, honey. We're on your dime."

MasquerAsiaN
I want to talk to you.

Her smile faltered for a second, but she recovered and smiled even bigger than before. She reached for the wipes he knew she kept nearby and began to clean up, averting her gaze from the camera. A small part of his heart hoped that what she was thinking in that moment was that she wanted to hear his voice; she wanted to meet him. Because he wanted that too. Even though it would inevitably be an absolute disaster and would certainly blow up in his face. But still… he wanted her.

"So are you going to tell me about your day?"

MasquerAsiaN

pink slip

Nothing to tell. I had a very boring day. A very boring few
weeks actually.
Tell me a story?

Typing didn't make the lie easier to tell.

She repositioned herself, facing the camera head on. He
missed the sight of her body, but the view of her cleavage was
nothing to sneeze at and there was something so innocent and
normal about the way her feet were raised in the air behind
her, her ankles crossing and crisscrossing as she spoke.

"Okay, so remember how I said I thought my neighbor
across the hall was cooking meth?" she asked, her voice
excited.

He smiled. Her neighbor wasn't. He'd investigated it. But
she'd turned into an amateur sleuth trying to figure out what
was happening, and he thought that was adorable.

MasquerAsiaN
I do. Are there new developments?

She reached one hand out and around the computer, off
screen. She was clutching her glasses in her hand when it
returned.

MasquerAsiaN
Oh you're bringing out the glasses? This should be good.

She slipped her glasses onto her face and nodded. "You
have no idea."

As she launched into the story, Kenny hoped that it
would run long because he would happily give her another
$250 to finish it and then come with her one more time.

He didn't know where he'd be in a week, what country or
on what mission, but wherever he was, he'd do whatever
necessary to make sure that he could block off an hour or two
to spend with her. Because, as he settled back against the

pillows and listened to her hilarious tale about the imaginary meth ring being run out of her apartment building, he was overtaken by the fear that this couldn't last. That it shouldn't last. And that if he knew what was good for him, he'd make this the last Thursday he spent this way. He'd thought the same thing last Thursday, and the Thursday before that.

"Sometimes you have control over a mission. Sometimes you don't," Monica had said when she and Lane were briefing him on Kierra's importance. He'd thought she'd been exaggerating then, uncharacteristically overcome with an affection for their former personal assistant. But he got it now. If there was ever a time when he could have walked away from Maya, it had long since passed.

The only thing that could keep him away from Maya, was Maya herself.

Acknowledgements

Pink Slip is a story I decided to write certain that no one would read it. And that was okay! I had such a vivid dream about Kierra, Monica and Lane that I wrote it (like a lot of my stories) primarily because it was a story I wanted to read. There are bits and pieces of me in all these characters and writing them made me happy in a moment when I wasn't. I've been completely shocked at how many of you have read it and recommended it to friends. You have no idea how happy that's made me, and I cannot thank you enough and if I could thank every single one of you I would.

I also want to thank Kai for helping me refine my vision, Jazmen and M for being such a great evangelists for this story and Nicole for reading literally everything I write because she's just that kind of friend.

If you liked Pink Slip, I hope you'll keep reading in the series. Maya and Kenny made me just as happy to write (even when I hated the story). I'd also really appreciate it if you recommended it to a friend who might like it and reviewing it wherever you feel comfortable. Also feel free to come talk to me on twitter @katrinajax! <3

Other books by Katrina Jackson

Welcome to Sea Port
From Scratch
Inheritance
Small Town Secrets
Her Christmas Cookie

The Spies Who Loved Her
Pink Slip
Private Eye
Bang & Burn
New Year, New We
His Only Valentine

Erotic Accommodations
Room for Three?
Neighborly

Heist Holiday
Grand Theft N.Y.E.

Love At Last
Every New Year

The Family
Beautiful & Dirty

standalone stories
Encore
Layover
Office Hours

CPSIA information can be obtained
at www.ICGtesting.com
Printed in the USA
LVHW091438090720
660236LV00003B/547

9 781718 019041